"Where to this time?"

"The Bahamas, then South America." There was the flash of smile over his expressive mouth. "Would you like to come with me, Miss Rose?"

"How could I take a leave of absence for a job I haven't started yet?"

One or two steps brought him close enough for her to feel the brush of his breath on her mouth. "You could, with the boss's permission."

She shook her head, hoping her heart wasn't in her eyes. Her lips parted to say that it was impossible, when his hands curved over her shoulders and she was impelled slowly toward him. His mouth touched hers, lingered, lifted, touched again. "*Au revoir*, Miss Rose."

LILIAN PEAKE lives near Oxford, England. Her first job was working for a mystery writer, employment that she says gave her an excellent insight into how an author functions. She went on to become a journalist and reported on the fashion world for a trade magazine. Later she took on an advice column, the writing of which contributed to her understanding of people's lives. Now she draws on her experiences and perception, not to mention a fertile imagination, to craft her many fine romances. She and her husband have three children.

Books by Lilian Peake

HARLEQUIN PRESENTS
1157—THE BITTER TASTE OF LOVE
1268—DANCE TO MY TUNE
1316—CLIMB EVERY MOUNTAIN
1485—IRRESISTIBLE ENEMY
1532—UNDERCOVER AFFAIR
1580—GOLD RING OF REVENGE

HARLEQUIN ROMANCE
2404—PROMISE AT MIDNIGHT
2603—NIGHT OF POSSESSION
2614—COME LOVE ME
2651—A WOMAN IN LOVE

LILIAN PEAKE

Stranger Passing By

Harlequin Books

TORONTO • NEW YORK • LONDON
AMSTERDAM • PARIS • SYDNEY • HAMBURG
STOCKHOLM • ATHENS • TOKYO • MILAN
MADRID • WARSAW • BUDAPEST • AUCKLAND

ISBN 0-373-11629-2

STRANGER PASSING BY

Copyright © 1992 by Lilian Peake.

This edition published by arrangement with Harlequin Enterprises B. V.

Printed in U.S.A.

CHAPTER ONE

As THE dinner progressed, so the noise level rose. As a result, Crystal was finding it increasingly difficult to communicate with the guests immediately beside her, let alone the people seated on the other side of the long, narrow table.

'I didn't realise,' Maureen Hilson was saying, leaning closer, 'that the Ornamental You group employed so many people.'

Puzzled, Crystal frowned. 'I thought you'd worked for them for years?'

'I have, but I've never seen so many guests here before. They must have opened new stores by the dozen in the last decade.' Maureen sounded worried. 'I hope they knew what they were doing. Sometimes,' she observed sagely, 'I think it's wiser to maintain the status quo, that is, not to expand, or, alternatively, to expand slowly and cautiously.'

'You mean,' Crystal commented, 'that sometimes small really is beautiful?' Maureen nodded, and Crystal went on, accepting a chocolate-coated mint sweet from the plate Maureen offered, 'If there are so many prize-winners it seems to me that it might bring down the value of the awards.'

Maureen laughed. 'These aren't all prize-winners, dear.' She took a sip of coffee. 'After all, there are the two of us, aren't there? If every shop has two—and re-member, as the manageress, I was offered another as-sistant in addition to you——'

'Which means,' Crystal put in, 'that some Ornamental Yous probably have a staff of three?'

'Right.'

'All the same, I wish you'd collect the award, Maureen,' Crystal urged. 'You're the more senior of the two of us.' After a mouthful of coffee she groped agitatedly for her glass, taking a mouthful of wine, then wincing at the resulting incompatible taste.

Maureen laughed at her expression. 'There's no need to be nervous, Crystal. I think it's better for the store's image to have an attractive young woman go up there and accept the award.'

'But——'

'Look, dear, all you have to do is smile, take the prize prettily, shake the hand that's held out to you and then it's over. Anyway...' they joined the assembled company, moving into the ballroom for an evening's dancing '...the awards aren't being made just yet, so for the moment you can forget your "ordeal", as you seem determined to regard it.'

Music of a soothing, after-dinner variety came from a group positioned on a platform at the end of the long room. Guests drifted into circles and Maureen became deep in conversation with an old acquaintance. Feeling a little lost, Crystal found a seat near by.

'Hi.' A bright-faced young man seemed to welcome the fact that she had joined him. 'You new?'

Crystal smiled. 'Yes and no. I was beginning to appreciate the meaning of the expression "lost in a crowd".'

The young man's hand came out. 'Roger Betts.' His clasp was firm, his brown hair cut short, his upper lip showing signs of an attempt to cultivate a moustache.

'Crystal Rose.'

Roger laughed. 'I like that. I can just imagine a rose made of crystal. I bet you're fragile.'

It was Crystal's turn to laugh. 'Sometimes, very.'

He looked at her with something more than interest. 'Where's your part of the world?'

'These parts. It just happened that the firm chose this area for the awards ceremony. Or so my manageress told me.' She looked at his round face, his slightly over-solid build, and guessed that he was tall. 'Do you work for Ornamental You?'

Roger nodded. 'But not in the retail side. I work at Head Office. I'm an assistant buyer—I help to select the goods you sell—plus I'm involved in looking for new sites for Ornamental. I've got ambitions beyond the retail trade, though. I'm taking a part-time university course in chemistry. I use my earnings to subsidise my studies.'

'How do you tie in your course work with your job responsibilities?'

Maureen had finished her conversation, noted with a pleased smile that Crystal was well occupied and moved away, only to be caught by yet another old friend.

'It's not easy,' Roger was saying. 'I spend almost every evening surrounded by textbooks. I write until my hand nearly drops off—then I drop off!'

'Wouldn't a computer or a word-processor help?'

He shrugged. 'It would, but I'd have to attend yet another course to learn how to use one. I must sound as if I come from the Ark—a bloke who's let modern technology pass him by.' His mouth went on a self-derogatory downward turn, but also, surprisingly, managed to smile at the same time. 'I'm one of those guys,' he went on, 'whose thoughts flow better from their brains to the paper via their hands, if you get my meaning, rather than being channelled first through a keyboard. You—er——' his eyes crinkled at the corners '—you haven't got one, I suppose?'

'A computer? I have, as a matter of fact. In my last job I worked with one, and when they updated they sold off their equipment cheap to their employees.'

'Oh, joy,' said Roger, brightening. 'You couldn't—um—wouldn't——?' Then he shook his head. 'Forget it. Your boyfriend would have my guts for garters, if you'll forgive the expression.'

'He can't,' she returned, smiling, 'because I haven't.'

'What, *you*—no boyfriend? I can't believe——'

'I did have, but——'

'Roger, you so-and-so,' an older man, shorter in stature and bespectacled, fisted him playfully on the arm, 'how're things?'

Roger clapped the newcomer on the back. 'Haven't met, have we, since the last Ornamental nosh-up? Meet my new friend Crystal—or,' with a grin, 'is it Rose?'

'Both suit,' said the other, shaking Crystal's hand. 'Hi,' with an appreciative smile. 'I'm Ted Field. Been with Ornamental long? Haven't had the pleasure of seeing you before.'

'Flatterer,' Roger remarked, waving a playful fist. 'I found her first.'

'That's OK, mate,' said Ted. 'I'm married, remember?'

'I've worked for Worldview for just under a year,' Crystal told him. 'Are you collecting a prize?'

'Nope,' Ted answered. 'Are you? Yes? What for?'

'Highest sales.' Roger nodded as if he knew.

'That's great!' exclaimed Ted. 'Ours have taken a——' With his hand he sketched a dive.

'Yeah, a lot of the other branches aren't that good, either,' Roger agreed, 'but Ornamental's got some way to go before we hit the rocks.' He held up crossed fingers.

'Roger, Ted...' Their attention was distracted, and Crystal took the opportunity to melt into the crowd. Maureen was in the centre of a chattering group, so Crystal made for the ladies' cloakroom to repair her make-up.

In front of the tinted mirror she pressed on a little powder, then smoothed the silky floral fabric of her skirt, straightening the belted matching top and fiddling with the chunky amber beads around her throat. Their colour, along with the amber earrings she wore, picked up one of the shades in her outfit and echoed the auburn warmth of her shoulder-length hair. This she combed, fluffing it out around her face.

'Hi,' a plump blonde young woman said to her reflection. 'You new here?'

Crystal answered the familiar question.

'That all?' The young woman's eyes dwelt enviously on Crystal's heart-shaped face. 'Wish I had your complexion. And your looks. They're just great. Your hairstyle suits your face. It's what's called oval, isn't it? And there's nothing wrong with your nose at all.' Ruefully she rubbed her own, which had a tiny turned-up tip. 'In fact,' she studied Crystal enviously, 'everything in your face goes with everything else, if you know what I mean. Lucky you. Not like me. My nose is the wrong shape for my cheekbones, and my chin's kind of quarrelled with my mouth.'

'Thanks a lot for the compliments,' Crystal answered, 'but you look more than OK to me too.'

'I do?' The girl looked down at herself and sighed. 'I keep dieting, but my extra inches must love me—they just won't leave me,' she tossed over her shoulder as she left. 'My name's Shirley, by the way, Shirley Brownley. What's yours?' Crystal told her. 'Crystal—nice.'

Following her out, Crystal found herself in a secluded corner of a lobby that led back into the ballroom. The whole tempo of the evening had, it seemed from her quick glance into it, speeded up.

The music had evolved from the soothing to the lively, and was plainly designed to bring couples on to the floor. A glimpse of the roving multicoloured beams that swung across then alighted on the gyrating dancers told Crystal that it had succeeded.

Feeling the extraordinary need to halt in her tracks, Crystal glanced around. Something, she felt with a curious shiver, was tugging at her, preventing her from joining the dancers. Her eyes were ensnared by two others, glinting pin-points of reflected light, owned, she saw, by a man who leant against a trellis-work threaded through with leafy sprays from a climbing plant.

On its way to his mouth, wrapped hygienically in a paper napkin, was a roast chicken leg, while beside him on a ledge was a pile of the same delicacy. Next to that was a partly empty bottle and a glass containing wine.

Crystal was only half aware of the man's repast, which he was plainly enjoying, since most of her attention was riveted on the man himself. He was tall and broad and business-suited, a faintly mocking smile highlighting a handsome, if slightly arrogant face.

She found herself moving towards him as if he were playing a line and she was caught by the bait on the end. Little by little, he reeled her in. This can't be happening to me, she thought, finding it quite impossible to free herself from his snare.

A few paces distant, she found herself pausing.

'Yes?' she heard herself whisper.

For heaven's sake, her rational self lectured, you've never seen him before. What are you doing, *talking* to a complete stranger, and a man at that, when he hasn't spoken a word to you?

He smiled, fully this time, and Crystal's heart did a kangaroo leap. Holding her eyes, he reached for the plate of chicken drumsticks and held them out. She shook her head, so he felt behind him for another plate, of savouries this time, offering these to her.

'I—I've eaten, thanks,' she managed, her mouth peculiarly dry. The plate remained extended. They looked so inviting, those savouries, that the appetite she had scarcely indulged during dinner because of thinking about her 'ordeal' to come became rekindled, and she accepted one with a murmured, 'Thank you, but——'

But what? she asked herself. He hadn't so far uttered a word. She had done all the talking. Go back to the ballroom, her reason urged as she consumed the savoury. 'Th-thanks,' she added as he thoughtfully passed over a paper napkin. Extract yourself from this incredible situation and pretend it never happened, her reason was commanding, badgering her mercilessly.

'Have another,' the man offered, adding as she hesitated, 'go on, spoil yourself.' Like a lightning flash speeded up, his glance raked her, then was gone. 'You have no need to worry about surplus weight.'

He had spoken at last! As if she had passed control of her reflexes over to the stranger, she took another, and he smiled, and once again she perceived that mockery was not far away.

'Didn't they feed you properly at dinner? You'll have to complain to the management.'

'I just wasn't hungry.' She frowned. 'Weren't you there?'

'I arrived too late. I've just flown in from North America—Canada, to be exact.'

'Ornamental You actually paid for you to take a trip to North America? I didn't think they were that generous—or so I've heard.'

'Excuse me.' He selected another drumstick with a fresh paper napkin, and proceeded to demolish it with a series of quick bites. 'I don't eat airline food,' he added between mouthfuls, afterwards adding a few savouries for good measure.

'Which means you must be starving!' she exclaimed.

His eyes did another quick, almost imperceptible reconnaissance of her person. 'I am. And you are——?'

'Crystal Rose.' A quirk of his eyebrow forced her on to the defensive. 'I have romantic parents.'

He laughed, and again Crystal's heart leapt. Who was this man that he could affect her so much?

Taking a handful of paper napkins, he cleaned his fingers and picked up his glass. Then he put it down. A tray of drinks passed within sight. 'You're not a tee-totaller?' he asked. As Crystal shook her head he beckoned to the waitress. 'Drink with me, Miss Rose,' he said softly, lifting himself upright and moving towards her. With his glass he touched hers. 'To the past. And to the future.' He touched hers again. 'May the two never meet.'

The wine was the same as that which she had drunk during the dinner, but it had miraculously transformed itself into nectar.

'What did your toast mean?' she heard herself asking as the wine decanted itself to every part of her. She finished every drop.

He put down his empty glass, taking hers. 'Dance with me, Miss Rose.'

It was more an order than a question. 'But I——' 'Don't know you,' she almost said, then contradicted her reason. *I've known him all my life*, she told it reproachfully.

Taking her hand, he led her into the ballroom and on to the dance-floor. The music had softened in quality, insinuating itself into the limbs, making them languid and flowing, the mind hazy. Yet Crystal found to her consternation that her heart was hammering, her skin jumping at the stranger's touch.

The lights swooped and selected, rested, then moved on. 'Why——?' she began, her throat oddly parched. 'Where——?' She tried again. 'Who——?'

His mouth took the law into its own possession, descending on hers, compressing, demanding, caressing, cutting off the question and momentarily robbing Crystal of breath.

Wide-eyed, she stared at him. Had there been a fleeting message in his dark gaze? Or something in his expression? Could it, she wondered, have been her subconscious mind linking with his, divining and intermingling with the thoughts that his contained? Or had it been someone passing and whispering to her? She didn't know, but from somewhere came the words, He's out of your reach ... Crystal broke contact and looked around. There was no one near them.

'You shouldn't——' she began, but those lips were back, tasting faintly of wine, playing with hers until they parted on an admonishing gasp, the arms around her having slipped to her waist. It was no use, she told herself helplessly, she was caught in this stranger's magnetic field—hadn't he used it to draw her to him?—and there seemed to be no way in which she could escape.

The music ceased, the dance ended. For a couple of seconds the lights were almost extinguished and only the dark outline of him remained. When they flashed on again he was gone.

The reappearance of food and drink put new life into the evening.

Maureen patted the seat beside her and Crystal joined her. 'So pensive,' Maureen remarked. 'Won't be long now, then you can relax. You found a dancing partner, then? The lights were so low that I couldn't identify the man.'

'I—what? Oh, yes.' With a jerk Crystal returned to the present. The stranger's arms still seemed to be holding her, the imprint of his mouth lingering alarmingly. 'I enjoyed it,' she added, quickly enough, she hoped, to avoid further questions, not wishing to talk about something that had become, quite foolishly, she realised, so precious to her.

A man materialised in front of her and her heart leapt, her eyes travelling upwards and bouncing disappointedly off the smiling face.

'Hi,' said Roger, holding out a plate and a glass of wine.

How *could* I have thought, Crystal reproached herself, that the stranger had come back to me? He hadn't been real; she'd dreamt him up out of her subconscious, she told herself. Wasn't she too old now to believe that dreams materialised, gained substance, *came true*?

'Thanks a lot,' she responded, accepting Roger's offerings. 'Just what I needed to boost my adrenalin for what's to come.'

'You won't believe,' said Maureen, 'that this girl's got butterflies because she's going on the platform.'

'I'm Roger Betts, by the way,' he told Maureen. 'There's nothing to it, Crystal. All you need to do up there is——'

'Shake hands,' Crystal put in with a laugh, 'and say thank you nicely. Maureen's already told me.'

'They're assembling on the platform,' Maureen commented, watching as various attractive-looking items were carried on and placed carefully on the long table behind which chairs had been placed.

Someone stepped to the front of the platform, hand raised for silence. After a few words of welcome and introduction he invited the prize-winners to assemble at the side of the platform. With Maureen's and Roger's encouragement ringing in her ears, Crystal followed the man's instructions.

From where she stood, she heard but could not see the line of company executives filing on to the platform.

'Know who all those guys are?' a young man asked her.

Crystal shook her head. 'I haven't been with the firm long enough to know.'

'Nor me,' the young man answered.

Short speeches were made in voices she could not identify.

'It is my pleasure to invite,' the man was saying, 'the chief executive of Worldview International, which is, as you all know, the parent company of Ornamental You nationwide, to present the prizes. Ladies and gentlemen, I give you Mr Brent Akerman.'

As the applause died down names were called, and one by one the people in the group around Crystal ascended the short flight of steps to the platform. The long wait, she realised, only served to increase her apprehension.

'Miss Crystal Rose.' Her name rang out, and it was almost with relief that she trod upwards, reaching the platform at last.

In a daze, Crystal walked on, head high, heart racing, and lost her hand in the firm enveloping grip of the man standing at the side of the long table. A smile was ready on her face, the phrase 'Thank you very much' waiting to be spoken, but her lips failed to co-operate and the words were never uttered. She found herself staring directly into the eyes of her dancing-partner.

His lips moved and Crystal knew he was addressing her, and she forced herself to concentrate on his words.

'Miss Rose,' he was saying, 'represents the branch of Ornamental You in this city. It is this branch that has achieved the highest sales of all. Miss Rose, we congratulate you and your manager, Miss Maureen Hilson, on your excellent achievement. You are both a credit to Ornamental You, not to mention Worldview International.'

With care he held aloft a crystal rose bowl, a beautiful object from which the light danced, refracting the colours of the spectrum. From all around there were sighs of admiration.

'Never has there been,' under cover of the sound came the words, to her and her alone, 'a more appropriate prize, both in name and in beauty.' Then the mask of detachment on Brent Akerman's face was back in place, the smile neutral and totally professional.

As if from a million miles Crystal heard the applause. Descending the steps, she sank on to the seat between Maureen and Roger. Wonderingly she gazed up at the man from whom she had accepted the prize. Had she really discovered him behind the scenes, quite unself-consciously devouring a scratch meal, which he'd offered to share with her? No, it just couldn't have happened.

On the other hand, she thought, although she hadn't invented the man himself, surely she had dreamed up everything else that had happened between them earlier that evening?

Yet, she pondered, if it had all been a dream, how was it that, when she closed her eyes, she could still feel the touch of his lips on hers, see the warmth of his smile and the moving lights reflected in his eyes? And in her mind experience all over again the incomparable sensation of dancing in his arms?

CHAPTER TWO

Two weeks later Crystal arrived, as she always did, half an hour before Ornamental You was due to open. For once Maureen was there before her, reading a letter, a frown creasing her brow.

'You've got one too, Crystal,' she murmured. 'I've been through this three times, but I still can't work out what it's all about.'

Crystal, experiencing an unaccountable feeling of foreboding, slit open the envelope that was addressed to her. Ever since Mick Temple's letter had arrived out of the blue two years ago, telling her that their friendship was over because he'd found another girl, Crystal's equilibrium had gone into the switchback mode every time an unexpected letter had come through her door.

But this wasn't her door she had just closed behind her, it was the shop's, which just had to mean that this official-looking communication in her hands meant business.

'What do you make of it?' Maureen asked, reading her missive yet again.

'"Your presence is required——"' Crystal read aloud '—note that word "required", not "requested"——' she pointed out '"—at a meeting of employees of the Ornamental You group of stores in Ye Olde Oak Tree Hotel, at seven-thirty p.m. on——"' She counted on her fingers. 'That's only two days' time. Too bad,' she replaced the letter in its envelope, 'if you're booked for that evening. Are you going?'

'Of course,' Maureen answered. 'It comes from Head Office. It's like a royal command, isn't it?'

'Oh, dear,' Crystal remarked, waving a feather duster over the varied stock displayed attractively around the shop.

'Why are you assuming,' Maureen returned, doing likewise, 'it's bad news? Might be the opposite.'

Crystal looked at the sparkling rose bowl that she and Maureen had won for highest sales. It stood in pride of place on a central revolving stand, the shop's lights angled so as to glance with brilliant colour off its many facets. She couldn't explain to Maureen, nor even to herself, why that letter they had each received seemed to bode ill rather than the opposite.

'You mean, an announcement of an expansion of the business?' Crystal asked. 'But didn't you tell me that they'd recently done that?'

'That's true. Oh, dear,' Maureen added as she turned the 'closed' notice to 'open'. The shop door pinged and two customers entered, wandering round.

'STAFF MEETING ORNAMENTAL YOU', the blackboard in the hotel's entrance foyer announced. 'WOODLAND ROOM. THIS FLOOR.'

Maureen entered first, peering round the door. Voices welcomed her by name, smiles and nods greeting Crystal. Most of them Crystal recognised from the prize-giving dinner.

Roger Betts stood and beckoned to them.

'You go,' said Maureen. 'I'll have a word with some of the others.'

Seats were filling fast as Crystal took her place beside Roger. 'Nice to see you again,' he said. 'I've been thinking of ringing you at work, but—well,' he coloured a little, 'I couldn't quite summon up the necessary cheek to ask.'

'Ask what?' she enquired with an air of innocence. As he looked even more uncomfortable, she took pity on him. 'Help you out with your notes, you mean?'

A brilliant smile lit his slightly sharp features. 'You could? You mean, you're willing...?'

She gave him an answering smile. 'I don't know, Roger. I'd have to think about it. OK?'

'You wouldn't be doing it for nothing,' he declared. 'I'd pay well—or as *well* as whatever's left over from my salary, anyway.'

Crystal shook her head. 'The money aspect doesn't worry me. It's——'

'Hi, Roger, and—Crystal, isn't it?' Ted Field stopped beside their row. 'Know what this,' he indicated the expectant-looking audience, 'is all about?'

'Haven't a clue,' answered Roger. 'Take-over bid for Ornamental? Who knows?'

'Oh, I hope not,' Crystal put in as Ted found a seat near by. Maureen bustled along to occupy the other seat beside Crystal, and quiet descended as the platform party made their entrance.

Crystal's eyes opened wide, her breath becoming trapped in her lungs. A man, tall and broad-shouldered, moved into the central position—a man grown familiar through his persistent appearance in her dreams.

His keen gaze swept the hall, passed across her, zipped back, rested on her for less than a second, then returned to his notes. Had he been *looking* for her? Of course not, she told herself, heartbeats racing, he wouldn't even remember her, would he?

So what if he had danced with her, kissed her under mixing, moving lights? She had been just another employee, someone who had appeared at exactly the right moment to act as undemanding subordinate while he had digested his meagre meal and coped with his jet lag.

Having disciplined her thoughts, she forced herself to concentrate on his brisk words of welcome. Listening to his voice, she found herself thinking how she liked its pitch, its tone, the melodious note that made her wonder if he possessed a good singing voice—or perhaps he had Welsh forebears?

'He can't mean it!' Roger exploded beside her. 'It can't be true.'

'What can't?' Crystal asked, hitting the earth with a bump.

'For heaven's sake, Crystal, haven't you been listening? Ornamental You—Worldview are closing us down!'

'Closing what——?' Then the penny dropped. 'It's not true!' she exclaimed. 'It can't be. Maureen and I—we're doing well. You must have misheard.'

'Misheard, my foot. They're closing them—us, all of us, he said.'

There were mutterings all around, heads turning to others, bodies twisting toward the rows behind.

'We, the management,' the speaker went on, 'very much regret the step we are having to take. We do realise that it will come as a severe shock to you all. We are extremely sorry,' Brent Akerman was saying, 'but I'm sure you will appreciate that, however much it might go against the grain, a loss-making chain, a non-profit-producing line of business, cannot indefinitely be allowed to go limping on by any parent company.'

'What about selling us off?' Ted Field shouted from the audience. 'That'd be better than what you—well, Worldview—are intending to do.'

'That was considered,' Brent Akerman took him up. 'We offered the chain of shops for sale, but, despite our great efforts, there were no takers.'

'Why weren't we warned?' a young woman asked, plainly near to tears.

Brows raised, Brent Akerman had his answer ready. 'This is your warning, which we considered was the gentlest method possible of informing you of the fate of the chain you work for.'

'What's gentle about this?' Ted Field queried.

Plainly impatient now, Brent Akerman replied, 'Would each of you have preferred to have received through your letter-boxes an impersonal note of dismissal? Or a cold-blooded few words in your pay packets—"Your employment is terminated as from today"? At least we've laid on drinks and a buffet.'

'Thanks a lot for that,' Roger half rose, 'but we'd rather have our jobs.' There was a general murmur of agreement.

'We at Worldview,' Brent Akerman went on, 'are giving you far longer notice of the termination of your employment than other firms, who merely announce their intentions to the media, or maybe take the trouble to gather together their staff on site and say, "Right, this is the end".'

He paused. His audience hung on his every word. A born orator, Crystal found herself thinking, at first with a curious kind of pride, then, as she caught up on her own thoughts, with a twist of resentment.

'The branch closures,' the speaker continued, 'will take place simultaneously one month from now. A generous redundancy payment will be made to every staff member,' with a fleeting glance in Crystal's direction, 'regardless of the length of their service.'

'I'm duly grateful for that,' Crystal heard herself saying, discovering, to her utter astonishment, that she was on her feet, 'but what I can't understand is why you're closing down all of us when, for instance, Maureen Hilson and I are doing so well at our particular branch.'

'Hush, dear,' whispered Maureen anxiously.

Crystal did not heed the warning. 'You . . .' she looked around, seeing faces as surprised by her outspokenness as she was, then swung her gaze back to the man she was addressing, recoiling a little at his irritated expression ' . . . you know that our branch achieved highest sales, because it was you who presented me with the prize. So couldn't you just—just——' her bravado, which she had never even known she had, was running out '—just be selective in your closures?'

'You mean,' he responded, his tone just this side of cutting, 'allow Miss Crystal Rose to keep her job, and fire all the rest?'

Her cheeks burned at his calculated sarcasm, even as her mind registered amazement that he had actually remembered her name.

'No, of course I don't mean that, Mr Akerman.' Was it really she, Crystal Rose, addressing the top man in that tone? 'I mean, couldn't you give *some* of us another chance, let us try to push up our sales before you shut down the whole chain?'

'It's an interesting idea, Miss Rose,' came the drawling reply, 'but the world of big business, of which you doubtless know only a minimal amount, doesn't make decisions based simply on hope rather than the distinctly disappointing, if not to say dismal, sets of figures put in front of it by their accountants.'

'Nor does it allow,' she retaliated, sweeping together the crumbs of her courage, 'for the human factor. I love my job, as I'm sure we all do here, otherwise this crowd,' she flapped her hand over their heads, 'wouldn't have bothered to show up. After all, the letter we received gave no indication of what the meeting was about.'

'*I* guessed,' said someone in the front row. 'Our sales have taken a shocking dive lately.'

'Ours, too,' said another man.

Crystal's heart sank. They all seemed intent on letting her down, yet if they were all speaking the truth... She would have to fight even harder, the employees as well as the management.

'So why have ours—Maureen's and mine—been so good?' she asked the meeting in general.

There was indulgent male laughter. 'Must have been a magnet somewhere in your shop that drew 'em in,' was one young man's comment, and he turned his head to get a good look at the lady speaker. 'A "hidden persuader", I think they're sometimes called in the trade.'

'In the form of a good-looking lady assistant,' another man qualified, 'who's got what it takes.'

On the platform Brent had taken the central seat, sitting back, arms folded, legs crossed, a smile lurking, seeming content to watch and wait, while his two colleagues appeared to share his barely veiled amusement.

Crystal shook her head, her auburn hair swirling around her shoulders. 'You're on the wrong track. Our stock appeals to young women—beads, bangles, headscarves, perfumes.'

'And what about the men?' Ted Field turned in his seat. 'Don't you get a single male in your shop?'

'Well, yes. Boyfriends, husbands...'

'All looking for gifts for the women in their lives. There you are, then. They see a pretty girl assistant and in they go.'

Crystal shook her head, bemused by the banter. 'But I'm——' I'm not that attractive, she had been about to say. She rounded on the members of the audience. 'I don't know how you can take it all so calmly. It's your livelihoods you're being deprived of, yours and mine. What about your families, your way of life? They,' she indicated the platform party, shutting her eyes to the increasingly darkening features of the chairman of the meeting, 'are threatening to take away your jobs, make you all unemployed——'

Roger's agitated hand tugged at Crystal's. 'Leave it,' he urged. 'You've said enough.'

'Yes,' whispered Maureen, 'he's right. Please, Crystal, sit down. It won't do us, or you, any good at all.'

Brent Akerman got to his feet. 'Not threatening, Miss Rose,' he grated, 'intending. Thank you for your intervention. I think your colleagues have provided the answers to your queries.'

Crystal was on her feet again. 'A management buy-out,' she exclaimed, 'that's what we want!'

'It's the *management*, Miss Crystal,' Brent Akerman clipped, with a mocking curve to his lips, 'who intend to close the chain. Don't you mean an *employee* buy-out?'

If his words had been intended as a put-down, he had succeeded. Cheeks hot, hand shaking a little as she smoothed back her hair, Crystal subsided, not completely sure as to just what had come over her. It must have been a side to her character that had been lurking below the surface for years, undisturbed and unprovoked, completely unknown even to herself, until that man, the man who stood on that platform so confidently, had prodded it awake.

More, she thought with dismay, he had prodded awake feelings within herself which she hadn't been aware of before and which, even as she gazed up at him, were making themselves felt only too plainly.

Maureen nudged her gently. 'That's good, that's very thoughtful,' she murmured.

'What is?' Crystal asked, coming, a little bewildered, out of her dream.

'Aren't you listening, dear? You really should be. They're giving us six weeks' pay over and above our notice, so that we can keep paying our bills and try and find other employment at the same time. And,' Maureen paused for effect even as Brent Akerman talked, 'they're giving us a very generous sum as redundancy pay.'

'In addition,' the chief executive concluded, 'we will do our best at Worldview to absorb back into the company, or into one of its subsidiaries, as much of the workforce as we can.'

'How's that for consideration?' Roger whispered in her ear. 'If they can find me only part-time work it'll help to fund my studies.'

Brent Akerman's hand waved to the long, laden tables that stretched down one side of the room. 'Having completed the unpleasant part of this meeting, I invite you all to help yourselves to the food provided.'

The platform party of three filed off, and as they did so Brent Akerman put his hand to his mouth to cover a wide, shuddering yawn. So he's bored to his core, is he? Crystal thought resentfully, following the others as they beat a path to the consumables. A small bar had been provided as a thoughtful postscript by the regretful, if unrelenting, Worldview management.

Crystal discovered that she was hungry, having had no time even for a scratch meal before leaving home. As she filled a plate and forked the delicious savouries into her mouth, others, doing likewise, joined her.

Maureen picked at the food on her plate, her mind plainly on other things. 'However will I manage without a regular wage coming in?' she asked the company in general.

'Find another job?' Crystal asked gently. She, like all the others, knew about Maureen's semi-invalid mother, who lived with her.

'At my age? And within cycling reach of my home, the way the shop is?' Maureen shook her head.

'Heaven knows,' Ted Field commented worriedly, 'how I'll manage to keep going financially. What did

you have in mind,' he turned to Crystal, 'when you suggested a buy-out?'

'Yes,' a rounded fair-haired young woman took him
up, 'have you got access to a gold-mine or something?'

Crystal recognised her as the girl who had spoken to
her in the cloakroom after the prize-giving dinner a fort-
night or so back. Shirley Brownley, she recalled, was the
young woman's name.

'I wish I had, Shirley,' Crystal responded, drinking a
mouthful of wine. 'But we could raise a loan, couldn't
we?'

'Anyone around here,' said Roger, grinning, 'got a
friendly bank manager?'

'Or a rich daddy?' asked Ted. 'And I do mean father—
nothing else,' he added as the others laughed.

'Mine's with my mother in Denmark,' Crystal declared, 'staying with old friends of the family. Anyway,
he took early retirement and he's anything but rich.'

'Oh, dear. So that's that idea knocked on the head,'
said Shirley.

'Let's try again,' Crystal urged. 'What about savings?
Couldn't we all pool them and——?'

'Mine are non-existent,' said Ted.

'Mine are sacrosanct,' Roger averred. 'They've got to
tide me over financially until I get my degree. Especially
as I'm now about to get the push.'

Most of the others seemed to be entirely in agreement
with him.

'Mr Akerman did promise,' Crystal ventured, 'that
those who weren't offered positions in the company's
other subsidiaries would receive good redundancy pay.
How about——?'

'Using that?' An older man shook his head. 'I'll need
mine to help pay the mortgage and keep the bailiffs at
bay.'

'Me, too,' chorused many of the others.

There the conversation tailed off, the group dispersing to help themselves to more of the food and fill their glasses with the surprisingly good-quality wine. This last, Crystal calculated, with unaccustomed cynicism, Worldview had surely provided not only to soften the blow of dismissal, but also to keep reality from bursting in before the doomed employees reached home.

Hunger appeased, she wandered somewhat despondently away from the crowd, finding herself in the open air and standing at the edge of a softly illuminated paved area set about with wrought-iron tables and chairs.

Other guests sat under the evening sky, some alone, others in cosy twosomes, plainly at one with the world, secure in their jobs and their ways of life. Unlike, Crystal reflected, herself and her colleagues, who had just been informed of their impending loss of employment and plunge into near-poverty, if not actual destitution.

Losing the job she loved and the salary that went with it was a double blow. It was money she needed to enable her not only to eat but also to pay the rent of the old but cosy two-bedroomed end-of-terrace cottage she lived in.

'Miss Rose.' Her name wafted, a mere whisper, on the cool evening air. 'Over here, Miss Rose.' Crystal swung towards a shaded corner of the wide patio from which the voice had come.

A figure half reclined against a plinth that supported the statue of a somewhat scantily robed woman rising with dignity and proud beauty towards the darkening sky.

The height of the man, the width of his shoulders, the elegant suit, not to mention the fine shape of his head and slightly indolent pose, told Crystal at once who he was. But should she go at his bidding? Her feet made the decision for her.

'Yes?' was her whispered answer as her closer proximity to him allowed her to survey the features she had come to know so well through their constant appearance in her dreams.

He seemed to have no answer to offer, except to hold out the dish of savouries he had selected from an assortment of edibles that rested on the statue's standing area. It was so reminiscent of the first time they had met that laughter tugged at Crystal's throat, and a brilliant grey-eyed smile echoed her amusement.

'I'm full, thanks,' she answered his gesture, but, as before, the dish was proffered again, so she accepted, and wondered at the strange improvement in the taste of the titbit on that of those she had eaten inside. It wasn't that the quality was better, she was sure of that. It was... what was it? The time, the place and the man standing there that had imbued the savoury with the flavour of nectar?

Should I, she found herself wondering, in view of the unhappy circumstances that now prevailed, really be on such—well, *friendly* terms with the top man? Wasn't she in danger of letting her colleagues down?

'You—you haven't just returned from a trip abroad, I suppose?' she queried, accepting—as before—the paper napkin he offered.

He nodded, consuming another portion of the minimeal as if he could not appease his hunger fast enough.

'I thought I recognised the signs,' she commented with a smile, which he returned, with a devastating effect on her pulse-rate. 'Your dislike of airline food?'

'Full marks for an excellent memory.' A sliver of salmon atop a bed of lettuce on a finger of toast was demolished by a crunch of formidable white teeth.

'Where—where from this time?'

He swallowed, licking his fingers then using a paper napkin, looking vaguely round for a waste-bin. Crystal took the scrunched paper from him, depositing it on a plate.

'Japan,' he just got out before another colossal yawn enveloped him. For a couple of seconds his eyes closed. Allowing himself a mere moment for recovery—his stamina, Crystal found herself thinking, must be remarkable—he reached across the plinth for a wine bottle.

Having secured it, he realised that, with the other hand holding a savoury, he had no hand free with which to pick up the glass that perched precariously on the stone base.

It took Crystal a mere second to react, seizing the glass by its stem just before it toppled. Taking the bottle, she poured him a generous supply. This he gratefully accepted, raising the glass in a salute and drinking deeply, his eyes reflectively on her as he imbibed.

Then they narrowed and she heard him ask, 'Who taught you to anticipate a man's needs so promptly and so skilfully?' The wine bottle was almost empty now.

'Instinct, intuition. Maybe my genes?'

A smile flirted with his expressive mouth at her playful reply.

'I,' he straightened, hands in pockets, 'would put my money on a demanding boyfriend.'

'Then, Mr Akerman, you'd be throwing your money away.' She didn't want to talk about Mick. It hurt even now, just thinking about him.

A reflective pause, then 'So keep off. I can hear it in your voice. OK, I won't trespass on private grief.'

'No, no, it's not like that!' And strangely, incredibly, it wasn't. Out of the blue, she discovered that she just didn't care any more about Mick Temple and the heartless way he'd thrown her over for another girl.

'So tell me, then,' he asked, ignoring her outburst, 'who taught you to be so belligerent and bellicose?'

Crystal's mouth fell open. 'You *can't* be talking about me?'

'Oh, yes.' Carefully he recorked the empty bottle. 'Who jumped to her feet this evening at every opportunity and challenged the platform?'

'Who——?' How could she tell him she had been as surprised as he was? 'Oh. I'm—er—sorry about that.' A pause, then, tossing her head, 'No, I'm not. What I said came from the heart.'

'Crys—tal? Hey, Crystal! So this is where you've got to.' Roger came round a corner and stopped dead, looking from one to the other, frowning uncomfortably. 'Sorry to butt in, but Crystal, I—er—we missed you. Thought you might have gone home without telling us.' With an apologetic lift of the hand, he made to leave, but checked himself. 'About that other matter, Crystal— could I call you, reference what we discussed?'

'Why not? Any time.'

Roger seemed pleased, and Crystal hoped he had not read more into her invitation than her agreement to do some office work for him.

'You'd better go, Miss Rose,' came the dry remark, Brent Akerman having plainly made his own—wrong— interpretation. 'Betts is missing you.'

Brent Akerman, the chief executive of the group known as Worldview International, actually remembered Roger's surname?

'The others, too,' he waved his hand vaguely, 'are missing their leader, their spokesman.' He folded his arms and leaned against the plinth, smiling mockingly. 'Oh, dear. Womankind will be after my——' an eyebrow darted upward '—be after me. I'd better feminise that word fast—*spokeswoman*. And,' his head went back to rest on the statue's hard bare thighs, 'do let the management know, won't you, if there's going to be a strike, or a sit-in? Or even a march in the town. You must inform the police about that, did you know? The management would hate to see the lovely Crystal Rose thrown into gaol through ignorance of the law.'

Annoyed by his cynicism, she was about to retaliate when she saw that his eyes had closed. 'Mr Akerman,' she whispered.

'Yes?' without lifting his head.

'Shouldn't you go home? I'm sure your wife will be anxious. Could I—shall I use the hotel phone and tell her you'll soon be on your way?'

'Call my place, by all means,' came from him harshly, 'but there'll be no answer. I have no wife, no clinging little woman waiting for me.' The bitterness was almost tangible.

'No one there?' Crystal asked, astonished that such a man, such a *masculine* man, had no woman in his life.

'No one,' he repeated, eyes still closed. 'I had my fill long ago of the "two hearts that beat as one" myth, of "devotion", and declarations of life-long love. There's a heart where a man's heart usually is, Miss Rose, but mine is ice right through.'

'It sounds,' Crystal offered into the taut silence, her own spirits unaccountably having taken a dive, 'as if you've been hurt very badly.'

'Does it?' he responded indifferently.

Eyes fluttering open, he pulled himself upright, swaying just a little. Crystal's hand on his arm steadied him and he looked down at it as if wondering how it had got there.

'I think, Mr Akerman,' she offered gently, 'that you might be just a little bit—intoxicated.'

'Think again, Miss Rose. The wine bottle was half full when I accepted it at the bar counter. One of the residents said he didn't want it and kindly offered it to me.'

'But you drank most of it on an empty stomach.'

'True. So?' The faint shrug and the light in his eyes convinced Crystal that most of his faculties were alive and well, if not entirely under his command. Then he swayed again. He swore under his breath and commented, 'I'm tired, Miss Rose, deadly tired.'

Crystal, hoping to humour him, tried reassurance. 'Jet lag probably, Mr Akerman.'

'Plus three late nights—or should I say early mornings?—in a row.'

'Are you going to drive yourself home?'

'Nope. I came here by taxi straight from the airport. If you'd call another for me, Miss Rose, I'll be eternally grateful.' His head was back against the statue, eyes closed again.

'Taxi, love?' the barman said. 'This time of night they're almost impossible to get hereabouts.' He indicated the wall telephone. 'But you're welcome to try.'

Someone was using the phone, which would mean a wait. So...*she* would take him home, in the car she had borrowed for the evening. Returning, she found him as she had left him, leaning, as still as the statue he rested against. Was he asleep on his feet?

'Mr Akerman,' her hand resumed its perch on his arm, 'this is the way outside. Will you come with me?'

With his eyes still closed he said softly, 'To the end of the rainbow, Miss Rose.'

His eyes opened and he looked straight into hers. It was like a bright light being switched on after intense darkness, and she found herself wanting to shield her own.

His gaze for once held no mockery, no warmth, yet no coldness either, but there was definitely a hint of something that sent tingles racing up and down her spine. Then his glance slanted down again at her hand. Maybe it was a presumptuous gesture, in view of who he was, but she had to get him outside somehow.

She had discovered a rear entrance that led on to the car park. Helping him into the front passenger-seat of the small car, she heard him mumble an address. Let him think it was a taxi driver he was addressing. He was too far gone, anyway, she reflected, pulling out into the road, to care whether his conveyance was a cab or a private car. She had caught enough of the address to let her know in which direction to point the car.

Rumour had it that he lived only a few miles from her own home town, so she drove in the general direction of the countryside but, dark as it was, with winding roads and hedges looming each side, and without his wide-awake directions, she felt as bemused as if she were lost in a maze.

Pulling in beside a farm gate, she called his name. He didn't stir.

'Mr Akerman!' louder this time, but she received the same response. Her hand once again found its way to his arm and she repeated his name, panicking just a little now. Her fingers walked down to his wrist, pressing the back of it. His hand turned over and captured hers.

'No, no!' she exclaimed, trying to shake free. 'Just tell me where you live, Mr Akerman. I need directions. *Please*, Mr Akerman.'

A long sigh issued from his lungs and he lifted her hand to his cheek. Oh, no, she thought, who does he think I am? His lady-love? There just has to be a woman in this man's life! She tried sliding her hand free, to no avail, so she changed tactics and jerked it away, hoping to wake him up. Her hand was relinquished, but to her dismay he settled into an even deeper sleep.

With a sigh of exasperation she turned the car and made for the town, pulling up at the rear of her little house, thrusting down her foot and braking sharply, but in vain. He stayed profoundly asleep.

CHAPTER THREE

THERE was no doubt about it: Crystal couldn't let Brent sleep in the car all night, so she took the only course available to her. Opening the door, she placed her hands on his shoulders and pulled. It was a miracle, but it worked: he did not resist. Instead, he moved towards her. Encouraged, she lifted his feet to the ground and managed somehow to manoeuvre him out, leaning him against the car. Diving round to lock it, she raced back, catching him as he began to slide sideways.

Lifting his arm across her shoulders and with her own arms around his waist, she urged him on beside her, he in a kind of waking sleep, she sagging a little under the weight of him. She was afraid that he might trip over the back doorstep, but he seemed to know by instinct that he should lift first one foot, then the other.

The sofa complained noisily as, hands on his hips, she guided him down. It was shabby, its springs almost flattened by years of wear, but its feather-filled cushions gave softly as she pushed them under his head, his shoulders and his calves. His height didn't help, his feet dangling over the raised arm, but it was the best she could do in the circumstances.

Looking down at him, she hoped he wouldn't be in too bad a shape when he awoke in the morning.

'If only,' she whispered, 'you'd been able to direct me to your own home, by now you'd be tucked up in your own comfortable bed.' There was no response, but then, she hadn't expected any.

It came two hours later in the form of the sound of furniture crashing and an unsmothered curse. The words, 'Where am I, for God's sake?' penetrated the ceiling of the living-room to her bedroom directly above.

Even if she had been sleeping heavily, which she hadn't, being subconsciously aware all the time of the presence of a stranger—and such a stranger!—in her small, normally quiet world, she would have heard him.

Swinging out of bed and tugging on a wrap, she tiptoed barefoot down the stairs and opened the living-room door, to find Brent standing, jacketless, bewildered and angry, beside the unfortunate table that had taken the brunt of his outflung, light-switch-seeking hand.

Diving to right the table and switch on the table lamp, she straightened to meet the furious grey eyes.

'What's this?' he growled, pulling at his tie as if it choked him. 'A plot among Ornamental's redundant employees to kidnap the chief executive with a view to working on him to change his mind and reinstate them?'

His gaze swept around, skimming over the tiny dining area, the spoof antiques, the badly worn carpet, plainly not liking very much what he saw, then tossed his discarded tie on to a bow-legged coffee-table from whose shiny surface it slipped to the floor. 'Where the hell am I?' he repeated.

'In my house, Mr Akerman. And if you'd let me explain——'

'So you——' he looked her up and down with as much pleasure in his eyes as when, moments ago, he had inspected his surroundings '—you, Crystal Rose, are their self-appointed spokesman, *yet again*?' His lips thinned. 'I might have known, should have guessed. Not only that, but also, because of your qualities of *leadership*, your *persuasiveness*——'

In vain, Crystal shook her head. Didn't he understand that that outcry on behalf of her colleagues had taken even her by surprise? That never in her life before had she sprung to her feet in the course of a meeting and addressed even the back of a person's head, let alone the platform?

'—they appointed you,' he was saying, 'kidnapper, abductor, hostage-taker in chief?'

This time her madly shaking head, the auburn lights of her mop of hair thrown around by the mock-crystal chandelier of which the cottage's owner was so proud, brought his accusations to a halt.

'If you'd just let me explain.' This time he heeded the appeal in her voice.

Having heard her out, he sank back to rest against the sofa. 'OK, I believe you,' was his weary response. 'This hangover is evidence enough. It was good of you to give me a lift. I see now that you had no alternative but to bring me here.'

'Jet lag,' she put in, 'not hangover.'

His eyes opened slowly, his gaze mocking. 'So many sides to the beautiful Crystal Rose. Chauffeur, minder, good Samaritan, political agitator——'

'No!'

'You mean, you're not beautiful?' Deliberately mis-understanding, Brent lifted his arms, resting his head on them. With an eyebrow arched, long legs stretched out, appreciation glinted in the faintly lustful gaze as it sketched her outline, which her thin cotton belted wrap did little to hide.

'No—I mean, yes. What I mean is——' An exasperated sigh came from the depths of her. 'Will you please stop referring to my defence of my colleagues' jobs this evening as evidence that I'm a revolutionary at heart? All I wanted was to safeguard their means of livelihood—people like Maureen Hilson, who's got an invalid mother to look after.'

'Caring as well as compassionate. I must look out your private file and make sure all these attributes are noted down.'

'What use will *that* be, Mr Akerman, when in a few weeks, along with all the others, I'll be an *ex*-employee of yours?'

'Mm.' Those dark eyes sketched a more intimate outline, shading in the curves and inlets like an artist sketching a particularly attractive piece of coastline. 'Play your cards right, Miss Rose, and——'

'*Goodnight*, Mr Akerman.' She swung to the door. 'Better luck with sleeping for the time that's left.'

He was on his feet and grabbing her before she had finished the sentence, and she hit the sofa beside him with a bump.

'I'm a stranger in a strange land, Miss Rose,' he declared softly. 'I'm shy.' His eyes held as many glints as the chandelier. 'I need reassurance—yours, as my hostess.' Laughter lurked as he whispered against her ear, making it tingle unbearably, 'I need my hand held, Crystal Rose.'

He took hers in a caressing hold, but loosely, so that all her hand needed to do was slip away from his. But it didn't. Perversely it stayed right there, liking so much the feel of his palm against its back, the strength of the long fingers that pushed their way between its own.

He then proceeded to unfasten his shirt buttons, placing her hand against his chest.

'Feel the way my heart's fluttering, Miss Rose,' he said huskily, 'it's jumping with sheer nerves at finding itself in the middle of the night in a stranger's house.'

There was the roughness of chest hair softening the hard breadth and sinew of him, but no sign of a quivering beat, only the vigorous hammering of the healthy heart of a jungle hunter in hot pursuit of its prey. The intimate contact of her hand against his flesh was electric, making her own heart flutter and dance in the most disconcerting way.

Her eyes collided with his, and to her consternation they could not tear themselves free. Laughter persisted in that grey gaze, mixed in with a predatory gleam, and a hint of very masculine desire. Not a sign of the shyness he professed to feel, but how could she have even begun to believe his outrageous statement?

'If I really believed you meant what you said about being shy, Mr Akerman,' she commented, 'I'd believe anything.'

She had meant it to come out with scorn laced with sarcasm, but she heard the catch in her throat, the quick intake of her own breath. He was having the same mind-blowing effect on her as he'd had from the moment she had set eyes on him.

Holding her gaze, he slid his hands to her shoulders, and before she was aware of his intention he had pulled her round and into his arms. Every particle of her knew she shouldn't be there, but her cheek had ignored all the warning signals and had taken the liberty of nestling cosily against the wall of his chest.

His arms held her loosely, but Crystal was certain that if she tried to escape they would clamp her to him without mercy.

'That's better, Miss Rose,' he sighed against her hair, 'much better. You're doing a great job of reassuring this timid guest of yours that his hostess won't bite him.'

Crystal laughed, then pulled back her head and searched his face. His mouth twitched and, flushing deeply, she disentangled herself from him. Yes, she had been right about the intended double meaning.

'That's not my way, Mr Akerman,' she declared, winding her wrap more closely around her.

He closed his eyes, legs outstretched, arms folded. Crystal gathered up the scattered cushions and placed them in a pile.

A shiver caught up with her, telling her how cool a night it was. She switched on the imitation coal fire that stood in the grate, then crept out to find a blanket, gently spreading it over him. Crouching down, she eyed his shoes. Dared she unlace them and ease them off? With her hand light as a butterfly on his knee, she scanned his features, and her heart turned over at the intensely unhappy expression on his handsome face.

She wanted to throw her arms round him to comfort him, easing the pain he was undoubtedly feeling. She wanted to offer him sympathy, ease away his sadness, soothe him with her warmth, *her love*...

Horrified by her thoughts, she made to rise, when a hand rested on hers on his knee. Mortified that he had known all along that her hand was there, she began to snatch hers away, when his hold tightened and he pulled her round and on to the sofa again.

His arm settled around her, and although she knew she should move away not a single nerve or bone in her body tensed to follow her mind's instructions.

His fingers tipped her chin and the glow from the electric fire lit her features, while his, to her chagrin, remained in shadow.

'When you looked at me, what were your thoughts?' he queried huskily.

So he'd seen her looking at him! And she had thought the light was so subdued and his eyes closed so tightly that her scrutiny of his face would have been a total secret.

'You looked so unhappy, Mr Akerman,' she answered softly, straining without success to read his expression, 'that I——'

'You wanted to apply first aid?' He shook his head.
'My emotions, my feelings—they're beyond repair.
Forget them. I follow my male instincts these days; my
emotions, where the act of love is concerned, are in cold
store, and there they'll stay.' Why, Crystal wondered,
had her heart just sunk like a stone? 'And you, Miss
Rose,' his slow kiss was a mere tantalising brush of the
lips, 'look pale and tired and in need of sleep. Put your
arm across my shoulders.'

Too weary now to disobey, she did as he had told her.
His arm enclosed her and her cheek found itself nestling
once more against soft masculine fuzz, while a rhythmic
drum beat reassuringly beneath her ear.

As her eyes closed she told herself that OK, so she
shouldn't really be there, that she should remind herself
of who he was and draw away, but for once she disregarded her powerful conscience and nestled even closer
to the man in whose arms she was drifting into a beautiful
sleep.

She found the note next morning. Sunlight shining in
through her bedroom window surprised her awake.

That's strange, she thought, I must have forgotten to
close the curtains last night. Then it all came back. No
strong arms held her, no gently breathing chest supported her head. She was back in her own bed.

Since she remembered nothing about climbing the
stairs, and she wasn't given to sleep-walking, there was
only one way she could have got there, and that was in
the arms of the person who had pulled the cover over
her.

Brent Akerman, removing her wrap and—she looked
down at herself—seeing far more than her outline beneath the lightweight fabric of her nightdress? She
blushed at the thought. But maybe she had dreamed that
Brent had held her close in the small hours?

Words, whispered in a beautiful speaking voice that she had heard but hadn't understood, came hazily back. She strained to make sense out of them, but they were just as mysterious now as they had been in the darkness. And the touch of lips on her forehead, the stroking disturbance of her hair—they, too, just had to be part of her dreams, because they'd never really happened. How could they?

Those murmured words...they still wouldn't let her alone. The way they had been spoken—hadn't there been a note of sadness, and yes, even of regret? Yet, if there had been, how could she have known when she had been sleeping so deeply?

The note was propped against a flower vase on a table near the main door. It said,

Crystal, thank you for your thoughtfulness in bringing me here. Thanks also for your hospitality.

And, almost as if in his mind he had whispered it,
Thank you for your warmth.

Brent.

CHAPTER FOUR

'HAVE you noticed?' Maureen Hilson commented that afternoon. 'Customers have been coming in in their droves.' She smoothed back her greying hair. 'I've hardly had time to breathe, let alone comb these beautiful locks of mine.'

'I noticed. What's more,' Crystal added happily, 'not only have people come in and looked around, they've also actually bought things.'

Maureen smiled, glancing at the rose bowl glinting attractively on a pink-tinted glass stand. 'I suppose you could say that we didn't get the prize for the highest sales for nothing.' She sighed. 'If only the company wasn't insisting on closing *all* the shops down. The chief executive—what did they say his name was?'

Crystal looked up from feather-dustering necklaces and picture frames. Did Maureen really not know? 'Akerman,' she informed her. 'Brent Akerman.' She rolled the names around her tongue, as they had been rolling around in her head almost every minute of every hour since she had slept in his arms. 'Brent', he'd signed himself in that note—and 'Crystal', he'd called her. She had put the slip of paper, which he had obviously torn from his notebook, in a drawer among her most treasured possessions.

'Mr Akerman—that's right,' said Maureen, mopping up some spilt liquid from the 'make up your own perfume' section. 'You—er——' She looked askance at Crystal. 'You wouldn't—er—have any influence with that very handsome male, would you, dear?'

Crystal swung around, duster held aloft. 'What do you mean?' Had she been seen ushering him, her hand on his elbow, through the rear entrance and helping him into her car? Had there been spies watching her house to note the time Brent had left?

Mentally she shook herself, telling herself not to think such melodramatic thoughts about a completely innocent situation.

'Well,' Maureen qualified a little defensively, 'Roger told us that when he looked for you yesterday evening he found you and Mr Akerman in a cosy twosome in a corner of the hotel garden.'

'Twosome? Myself and the chief executive of Worldview International?' Relief made Crystal smile. 'Roger's got to be joking!' She added truthfully, 'Mr Akerman was telling me how jet lagged he was, that's all, and how often he—well, commuted on business to other parts of the world.'

Maureen nodded. 'Ah. I thought Roger was making too much of it. Crystal, dear, I think he's jealous. I'm sure our Roger fancies you.'

'Oh, no,' Crystal returned, dismayed. 'It'd spoil our business relationship if he does.' Seeing Maureen's puzzlement, she explained, 'He's a nice bloke, but if he tries to get more than friendly I won't be able to keep my promise to help him out with his written work.'

'What's wrong with him, Crystal? A lot of girls would love to have him around.'

'Yes, well, I'm not one of them. I've had enough of the opposite sex for a long time to come. The man I thought for months was *the* one for me called me on the day he'd promised to buy me a ring and told me he'd found someone else. It'll take me a long time to trust another man the way I trusted Mick Temple.'

'I understand how you feel,' Maureen sympathised. 'I met him once, remember, when he called to take you to a meal.' She shook her head. 'I could sense that underneath that smooth talk he was a no-gooder.'

After a reflective pause Crystal went on, 'Anyway, even if I'd had any influence with the chief executive, what good would it have done?'

'It's just that I was going to suggest you might ask him to make an exception of our branch of Ornamental You. Especially as our sales figures outdid everyone else's.'

'You mean, ask him to allow this branch to continue to trade, but close all the others down?' Crystal shook her head. 'I don't think it would be practicable. And I don't think for a minute that he'd even consider it. You'd realise what a hard man he really was if you'd heard him talk as he talked to——' She pulled herself up sharply. 'Talked to me last night about his private feelings,' she had been going to say.

'Of course,' she amended hurriedly, 'you did hear him speak, didn't you? At the meeting yesterday evening. Well, there was no "give" in the man, was there? Only the tired old "this hurts me more than it hurts you" routine.'

'Ah, well.' Maureen shrugged disappointedly. 'It was just a thought. Although how I'm going to provide for my mother as well as myself when I lose this job, I just don't know. As a semi-invalid, she needs so many little extras to help her. Also, jobs don't exactly grow on trees these days.' She sighed. 'All the same, you'd think it would count, wouldn't you? After all, you and I—we did——'

'Achieve the highest sales,' Crystal took her up sympathetically. 'I don't know how I'm going to be able to pay my rent, but, unlike you, I've only got myself to worry about.'

A group of young women entered, asking each other's advice as to what to buy. Then they consulted Crystal and Maureen. As they left with their purchases one of them said, 'We saw a report in the local paper that all the Ornamental You shops are closing. Is it true? Because if it is it'll be a real blow.'

'It's true, I'm afraid,' said Crystal sadly.

'Well, we're at college, and dozens of us come here to buy birthday and Christmas presents because your prices are so reasonable compared with other stores.'

'Hey,' said another, 'let's get together, girls, and try and scrape up enough cash to buy this shop.'

Filing through the door, they laughingly agreed it was a good idea, although one commented, 'Count me out. I've hardly got a big enough grant to keep myself in food and textbooks, let alone going into the red through trying to move into big business!'

'Now that's an idea,' declared Maureen when they had gone. 'If you and I pooled our savings... No?' as Crystal shook her head. 'No, I guess not. But the idea's a good one.'

Other customers drifted in, and by the end of the day Crystal and Maureen were delighted to discover that their takings were higher than ever.

That evening, tucking her aching feet beneath her, Crystal curled up on the sofa she had shared with Brent and for the twentieth time read the note he had left for her.

What if she took his words at face value? It then became a straightforward thank-you note, which she supposed was perfectly reasonable in the circumstances.

On the other hand, if she allowed herself to read not only between the lines, but also between the *words*, especially that last sentence, the slip of paper acquired a glow, the note itself becoming heavy with hidden meaning, with unspoken declarations of love...

Admonishing herself for her sentimentality, for sheer stupidity in embroidering the facts until they became the stuff of fiction, Crystal put the note aside. Then she took it up again and held it in case it blew away in some errant draught.

Head back, she felt her wayward thoughts conjure up the feel of Brent's arms around her, the brush of his lips across hers... Her common sense brought her sharply back to the present and she began to wonder...

Would Maureen's idea of her making a last-minute appeal to Brent Akerman have any effect? Would their more than close encounter last night make him more willing to listen to her and perhaps put him on their side? After all, sleeping in a man's arms, even though she had only been seated beside him on a sofa, must surely count for something more than if she'd merely been on nodding terms with him?

She seized a cushion from behind her and hugged it close. 'Mr Akerman,' she could say, 'it's been suggested to me by Maureen Hilson, my colleague—and I thought it was a very good idea—that you might allow...the company might allow...'

Yes, that should be OK, but how to contact him? By post? Or maybe she could fax a letter? The father of one of her friends had a machine in his home for business purposes. No, sending a letter that way would be too risky. If someone saw the faxed copy and discovered what she was trying to persuade Brent Akerman to do—save one shop from extinction, even though all the others were closed down—it might well stir up trouble and also damage her case immeasurably.

Should she ring Head Office and ask for him personally, taking the risk of being snubbed by his secretary? *Or should she go and see him?*

See Brent Akerman again? Her heart leapt, then dived. The chief executive of Worldview International wouldn't even consider setting aside two minutes, let alone half an hour of his time to discuss what would be to him such a trivial matter.

Plumping up the cushion, she turned to replace it when her eye caught a glimpse of a piece of patterned material that seemed to have partly hidden itself beneath the sofa.

Crystal extracted it with care, holding it up.

Before her startled eyes the tie Brent had been wearing the evening before unfolded itself. He had, she remembered, removed it in the course of those hours they had spent together, the thought of which even now made her pulse-rate accelerate. After dropping the tie he must have accidentally pushed it under the sofa.

Now she had a reason for seeing him again. So what if it might be simpler to push it into an envelope and post it to him? But that was something she couldn't do, because she didn't know where he lived. Nor could she send it by post to his office. She imagined the expression on his secretary's face as she opened an envelope addressed to her boss, only to find that it contained a folded tie that belonged to him. And that it had come courtesy of one of the firm's lady employees!

Crystal picked up the phone next morning. 'Maureen, I'm going to take up your suggestion. About Worldview making an exception of our shop.' The fact that she would also be returning Brent's tie was a secret she would keep forever. 'Yes,' she went on, 'I'm going to try to storm the bastion—Head Office—and fight my way through to the boss of bosses——'

'It'd be simpler,' Maureen commented with a laugh, 'to use your charm. Roger was only saying the other evening—"Has that Crystal Rose got charm...plus!" he said.'

Crystal turned pink at the compliment, but shook her head. 'He only said that because I've agreed to help by typing his work for him.'

'I doubt it, dear. Look in the mirror and you'll see what he means. If you used it the way other women do,' Maureen pursued her theme, 'it could open all kinds of doors for you.'

'Maureen,' Crystal exclaimed heatedly, 'I hope you're not insinuating that I should try and *seduce*——'

'Mr Akerman?' Maureen laughed again. 'Not likely! Not you. Charm you may have, dear, but you haven't got the slinky sophistication he'd want in his women.'

What you don't know, Crystal wanted to say, and what no one will ever know, is that I slept in his arms the other night...

Crystal had warned Maureen that she might be late in, but, as it happened, she was not.

'Didn't you get anywhere?' Maureen queried sympathetically, seeing the disappointment in Crystal's face.

'The first time I tried he was in a meeting, or so they said. The second time I was told he'd gone to keep an appointment. Helen Cooper—that's his secretary—asked if she could give him a message. I gave my name, that's all. What else could I do?' Her shoulders drooped as she closed the cupboard door on her jacket. 'I don't suppose my call will even reach him, let alone my name. Anyway,' she squared those shoulders now, 'even if I'd got around to mentioning the reason for my call, I'm sure he'd have laughed me off the line.'

'Mustn't be defeatist, dear,' murmured Maureen as a customer came in.

Mid-morning the phone rang in the small office at the back of the shop. Maureen answered. 'Miss Rose? Yes, Mr Akerman, she's here.'

Heart racing, Crystal took the phone. At home she had rehearsed her little speech so carefully. She had even made some notes, but she'd left them behind on the hall table.

'Yes, Mr Akerman?' Did her throat have to sound so hoarse?

'You're asking me why I'm calling, Miss Rose?' Amusement lurked in his voice. 'I'm calling to ask you why you called *me*.'

Which, her reason told her, was only fair, wasn't it?

'It's just that I wanted to ask you . . . I'd like to request that . . . would it possible for you—no, the——'

'*Please*, Crystal,' hissed Maureen from the doorway, 'use your charm. You won't get anywhere with him unless you——'

A customer cleared her throat loudly and Maureen left to attend to her.

'Are you alone?' Brent asked.

'I am now.'

'I guess I know, Miss Rose,' and Crystal could swear that his voice held a softer note, 'why you want to see me.'

Only one of the reasons, she thought. 'I'd have put the—the object in the post, Mr Akerman, but——'

'For God's sake, don't do that!'

'Of course I won't. I haven't got your home address, and if I send it to your office your secretary might——'

'OK,' came his cut-off reply. There was the sound of fingers drumming. 'Leave work early tomorrow afternoon, and meet me, will you, at the Gemini Palace Hotel at seven?'

'In London, Mr Akerman?' And such a hotel!

'Take a taxi, Miss Rose, if you find the train timetable too complicated to read.'

The sarcasm made her bristle. 'Money might come in trunkfuls to you, Mr Akerman, but to someone like me——'

'Are you asking for a pay rise, Miss Rose? And after you've received your dismissal notice, along with all the others, too?'

He was baiting her, and she would not take it... She heard a groan behind her. 'Use your charm, Crystal,' Maureen urged again, 'for my sake and my mother's.'

Maureen was right. Although Brent Akerman's sardonic amusement at her expense might make her want to hit him, or at least crash the receiver down, she swallowed her pride and her retort. She wanted something from the man and so did Maureen, which meant, didn't it, that she, Crystal, had to curb her desire for verbal revenge?

Brent broke into the merry-go-round of her rebellious thoughts. 'The company will bear the cost of the taxi ride. I'll look forward to seeing you,' he spoke the business jargon crisply. 'Seven prompt tomorrow evening.'

CHAPTER FIVE

BEMUSED, and just a little bewildered, Crystal paused. The entrance lobby of the Gemini Palace Hotel was extensive and full of bright, loud-voiced people. Everyone seemed to be at home in such an extravagant milieu, Crystal observed, except herself.

Ornate illuminated fountains featured giant open-mouthed fish, spattering the unwary, shedding a beguiling glow on to the décor and, as if they enjoyed the joke, on to the faces of the guests milling around.

Yet again Crystal opened her handbag to check that Brent Akerman's tie was securely tucked away. With as much nonchalance as she could muster, and that was infinitesimal, she walked, head high, across the lushly carpeted foyer and tried to lose herself in the list of companies whose conferences were currently being held at the hotel. In vain—and this puzzled her—she searched for Worldview International's name.

She was too excited at being in such a place to be able to concentrate for long, and her attention strayed. She might as well, she decided, make the most of finding herself so unexpectedly in the luxurious ambience of such a place. Financially speaking, hotels like this simply didn't appear on her visiting list.

She needn't stay long, she reflected. She could enquire as to the whereabouts of Brent Akerman, and if she discovered that he had decided, after all, not to waste his time waiting for one of his employees—one who was already on the redundancy list—hand the small package over to be given to him and leave. Maybe that was what he had in mind? In which case, she accepted ruefully, all her efforts to look both businesslike yet fashionably casual had been wasted.

Not that it mattered, of course. She rehearsed in her mind the sequence of events. On seeing her across the foyer—if indeed he hadn't left the premises—he would excuse himself from his guest's side—in such a place he would surely have a glossy, sultry female in tow, even though he might only be there for business reasons—and approach her, Crystal Rose, his hand extended for the package he knew she was bringing.

Then, with a polite smile, he would express his thanks and dismiss her with a nod. If so, she would have lost nothing. Not only had she not bought a new outfit for the occasion, he had also promised that the company would bear the cost of the taxi ride.

The fountains fascinated her, the curving sprays changing colour in the varying underwater lighting. A chance draught made them drift her way, dampening her hair and face, not to mention her jacket and skirt.

Gasping at the sudden drenching—she could have sworn that she heard the ornamental fish laughing—and blinking to rid her eyelashes of the clinging waterdrops, she raked in her bag for a handkerchief, becoming aware that someone was standing beside her.

'I'm fine,' she managed, 'please don't worry——'

A square of soft cotton was pushed into her hand and a familiar voice commented with irony, 'Want to sue the management for half drowning you?'

She swung round to find Brent Akerman looking down at her, his smile faintly mocking. He retrieved his crumpled handkerchief.

'On second thoughts, Miss Rose, since you're my guest, I'll do the mopping up.' He patted her cheeks dry, then ran his hand over her hair. 'What's wrong?' as she

tried to stop him. 'Am I messing up your hair-style?'
He just went on stroking her amber curls.

'Please...' She stepped back, but fingers almost as
tight as a tourniquet closed around her arm.

With a frown bordering on anger, he pulled her against
him. 'Are you really trying to drown yourself in the hotel's *pièce de résistance*? One more step and you'd have
executed a swallow dive backwards.'

She had forgotten that the pool was only a step away!
His gaze locked with hers and unaccountably her legs
assumed the consistency of melting ice-cream, while at
the same time her heart danced a jig. 'S-sorry about that,'
she managed, 'and thanks for saving me.'

Whenever she was near this man, he did something
to her, something she had vowed, after Mick Temple,
never to feel again for any man. There was only one
thing to do—hand over the tie and turn and run... out
of his orbit, out of his magnetic field, out of his life—
because when would she ever have reason to see him
again?

She forced her eyes from his and produced the packet.
He nodded and pushed it into his pocket.

'Goodnight, Mr Akerman.'

His hand wrapped around her wrist as she made to
move away. 'Where the *hell* do you think you're going?'

Crystal looked round wildly, her heart tripping over
itself at the grip of his long, strong fingers. Where was
that sleek lady companion of his she had dreamed up?
Nowhere in sight, but almost certainly dressing herself
in his hotel room. She gazed up at him, her eyes sliding
over the jaw which had been shaved smooth surely only
half an hour before, and now thrust out with displeasure.

'Your guest—she'll be expecting you back.'

'What guest? And who is "she"? Miss Rose,' with a
long-suffering sigh, 'there is no "lady". You are my
guest. There's a table reserved and waiting for us.'

'But Mr Akerman, you didn't say anything about inviting me to dine with you.' She looked down at herself, wishing she had chosen her clothes with even greater care.

'No? The implication was there, surely. Most women take it for granted that their host will feed them in style.'

'I'm—I'm not like "most women",' was Crystal's rejoinder as she wrenched her wrist free of his grip and rubbed it back to life.

'You can say that again! I guess I should have remembered,' eyes hooded, expression unmistakably sensual as he looked her over, 'that Crystal Rose is a law unto herself. Drink, Miss Rose?'

He cupped her elbow, leading her towards the semicircular bar. He had taken her agreement for granted, ordering for her, but somehow the arrogance in his assumption that she would like his choice did not rile her as it would in any other man. He had guessed her preference, anyway.

'Take a seat. Make yourself at home, Miss Rose.' She swallowed a gasp as his hands closed around her waist and lifted her on to a high stool. 'Be a devil,' he said softly, still holding her. 'Loosen up and behave like a lady being taken out for the evening.'

How can I, she thought agitatedly, how can I even think straight when you're holding me like this? 'I—I'm not accustomed——'

'To finding yourself in such glittering places?' He dropped his hands, but his eyes mocked her. 'Doesn't your boyfriend indulge you sometimes and——?'

'I've already told you——'

'No boyfriend.' He turned his attention to the bar assistant, giving his room number and signing a chit.

He lifted his glass, touching hers. 'Here's to travelling light all our lives.' Leaning sideways against the bar counter, glass in hand, he added softly, 'Know what I mean, Miss Rose?' How was it that whenever he spoke her name it sounded like an endearment? 'You and I, two of a kind, unlucky in love. Yes?' He drank, looking at her over the brim.

'Yes.' She frowned and looked away. Why did Mick Temple's rejection of her not matter any more?

'Did he hurt you that much?' Brent asked softly.

She took a drink. 'I survived, thank you.'

'You live to love again?'

'No!' It had come out too quickly, too emphatically. She was afraid to look into her heart and give the real answer.

He tossed back his drink and thumped the glass down. 'As I said, two of a kind. Life without love, Miss Rose, that's the best scenario. For both of us.' The bitterness came through loud and clear. 'Yes?'

No! she wanted to shout. 'Yes,' she answered quietly as he helped her down.

'Did I thank you,' he asked over dinner, 'for taking the trouble to return my tie?'

'It wasn't any trouble. After all, you paid for my transport, and you've treated me to this wonderful meal.'

'You regard this,' he indicated the table, the surroundings, 'as a reward for coming?' He added with a provoking smile, 'I thought that the least you'd demand in return would be, if not a directorship, then an about-turn in the company's decision to close down Ornamental You.'

The idea of pleading with him hadn't been far from her mind! Was this the opening she had been hoping for, which Maureen, as she had waved her on her way, had said she was desperate for?

Sipping some wine to moisten her parched mouth, and for courage, she said, 'Mr Akerman, I——'

'Crystal...' he waited until she lifted her eyes to his '...you've danced in my arms. My lips,' his fingertips touched them, then hers, making her shiver, 'have made themselves familiar with yours. Also, a couple of nights ago, you slept in my arms. Don't you think it's time you called me by my first name? Say it.'

His gaze shone in the candle-light, hypnotising her.

'Brent,' she obeyed his command.

When he extended his hand palm upward across the table she found herself unable to resist the invitation. His fingers closed over hers and he murmured, 'Good to meet you, Crystal.'

She smiled at his 'introduction' and did not want his hand to let hers go. The waiter approached and Brent released her.

Whisking away their sweet dishes, the waiter asked, 'Coffee in the lounge as usual, sir?'

'As usual.' Remember that, she told herself. Don't forget those 'other women' he talked about.

In his position in life, he must have entertained many to dinner, most of them, she'd like to bet, being members of her own sex. Had they felt as she felt now—cherished, admired and glowing inside?

Of course they had. He was clearly a master of the art of making a woman feel appreciated, attractive and, most of all, desired. So stop it, she chided her emotions, stop believing that he regards you as more than just another dinner date. He's playing with you, just as Mick Temple did.

Seated at her side on a low settee, Brent invited her to pour. As she handed him his cup, receiving a smile that made her heart disobey her orders and dance again, she thought, I'm sure *this* is the chance I've been waiting for.

'Brent——' she began.

'Hi, there, Mr Akerman. I didn't see you at breakfast this morning.' The young woman, in her cleverly casual clothes, looked only at Brent, her eyes eating him.

Brent smiled his charming smile and stirred his unsweetened coffee for an unnecessary length of time.

'Hi, Samantha. I used room service.'

'Sammy to you, Mr Akerman.' She drew her gaze around the solid outline of him like an artist taking mental measurements. 'Oh, don't do that often, will you, Mr Akerman? I miss you when you're not there. Heaven knows,' her eyes flipped ceilingwards, 'there are few enough attractive guys around to feast your eyes on first thing.'

She left with a wave, and there was a small, brittle silence. 'One of your—er—admirers, Mr Akerman?' Crystal ventured with a crooked smile.

'One of many,' was the sardonic, self-mocking reply. 'And before her appearance on the scene it was "Brent".' A quizzical eyebrow lifted in her direction. 'You were saying?'

Nothing for it now but to plunge right in. 'About the proposed close-down of Ornamental You——'

'Intended,' he corrected crisply, 'and, to make use of an old cliché, I never mix business with pleasure.' He pushed his cup towards her and she poured, returning it to him with a shaky hand.

The comment was plainly meant to end the discussion before it even began, but she just couldn't let this opportunity slip through her fingers.

'But Mr Akerman—I mean, Brent...' If her uncertainty showed she didn't care. If he was unwilling in such a situation as this—her eyes flicked around the lush environment—to discuss the subject closest to her heart it meant that she would have to confront him in his office, and her mind flinched just thinking about the power he wielded. Seated relaxed at her side and speaking in such resolute tones, he was alarming enough. Behind a desk he must be formidable indeed!

He drank, tilting his head. The mere sight of his dark jaw and throat where evening stubble was pushing through, despite an earlier shave, had a devastating effect on Crystal's equilibrium.

'Let it go, Crystal,' he warned softly, reaching forward to put down his coffee-cup.

'I—I can't, Brent. Too many people are depending on my efforts. Have you even considered the hardship you'll be inflicting——?'

'Are you trying to argue that the redundancy package isn't good enough?' No charming smile now, no lips curved in amusement, only a tight line and narrowed eyes.

'No, but——'

He got to his feet. 'If you're determined to act the union leader *and* the rebel we'll go up to my room.'

'I'm not; I'm not, Mr Akerman—I mean, Brent! I've never taken part in a strike or rebellion in my life.'

'Then don't start now, sweetheart.' He stretched down and seized her hand, pulling her to her feet. 'This way. It's on this floor.'

He was taking her to his room? 'Mr Akerman— Brent—I have to go.' She tugged hard, but his hand gripped hers like a vice. 'Thanks so much for that delicious dinner. My—my train, I'll miss it if I——'

'You know darned well, Crystal,' his key card operated the room lock, 'that your taxi fare back will be paid by me.'

'So why——?'

He pulled her in, releasing her at last. The room was a suite with a sumptuous living area, into which they walked. Behind a closed door no doubt there was a bedroom and a bathroom. It must have cost a small fortune, Crystal reckoned, glancing round wide-eyed, to hire it even for a couple of nights.

'It—isn't it——?'

'Luxurious, charming...ostentatious?'

'No, no, I——'

'It's my home, Crystal.' He pocketed his hands. 'It's where I live.'

She frowned. 'You don't have a real home? I mean, a house?'

'A roof over my head? A place I can call mine? No, Crystal. Does that touch your caring heart? Rich man, but beggar man where love's concerned?'

Strangely, it did, but she gestured to the lavish comfort. 'It's wonderful to be given a chance to see such a place.'

He stood squarely in front of her, deliberately intimidating, she was sure.

'You've dented my ego, Miss Rose,' he declared, brows drawn but with mockery in his gaze. 'I thought you'd agreed to dine with me because you couldn't resist my manly charm.'

He was right, she couldn't! But, if it killed her, she'd summon all her strength, both mental and physical, and do just that.

'You were asking why,' he reminded her. 'So come on, why what?'

'Well,' she just had to continue now, 'why did you bring me up here when you've just placed an embargo on my even mentioning the—the subject I started to talk about earlier?'

His gaze became a touch sensual as it slid over her shapeliness, returning to rest enigmatically on her face. 'I'm beginning to wonder that myself.' He turned away, staring out at the fantastic view over London that the uncurtained windows afforded.

So he wasn't attracted to her? She didn't affect his masculine reflexes as she appeared to do Roger Betts's?

'If I'm not dressed to your liking, Mr Akerman,' burst out of her, to her horror, 'if I fall below the sartorial standards you set for whichever woman you decide to be seen with for the evening, I'm sorry, but——' she couldn't stop now, she was too angry, too disappointed...about what? a small voice asked '—I don't have the financial resources that your lady companions no doubt have. And I'm about to lose my job, along with dozens of others——'

He swung around, eyes blazing. 'There's only one way,' he ground out, 'to silence your revolutionary fervour,' he gripped her shoulders, then slipped his arms around her, 'and that is this.' His hand fastened around the back of her head, giving her no chance to evade him.

His kiss was profound, invasive and shattering. When he lifted his mouth from hers he stared into her eyes, watching unmoved as she fought for breath. Her eyes must have revealed to him her confusion, her astonishment and disbelief, but, in his, fire fought with ice. She made to pull away, trembling, and saw that the fire had won.

He changed his hold so that she was cradled. His mouth lowered again and the kiss he took from her this time was so warm, so caressing...so stirring, so exciting that Crystal found herself responding in a way that in a saner frame of mind would have horrified her.

He muttered inaudible words against her mouth, pushing off her jacket and letting it fall. He moved her a few paces backwards and she was powerless to stop him. He lifted, then lowered her to a sofa, following her down. Sirens began to shriek inside her head. Stop this man, you mustn't let him, not like this...

She couldn't hear the warnings for the mad beat of her heart, for the delight of her senses at the pressure of his body on hers and all that that might lead to, regardless of the consequences. When his hand found her blouse opening, and pushed its way in to cup and caress her breasts, flashing lights were added to the sirens' wails and she began to fight him off.

He froze, waiting. At last he raised his head. 'Is it yes? Or no?'

She closed her eyes, shutting him out. 'No,' she whispered hoarsely.

Without a word he lifted himself upright. She heard him move, and opened her eyes to see him pushing the tie she had returned to him into a drawer. Slowly she sat up, refastening her blouse while he rang Reception for a long-distance taxi.

Her hands were trembling so much that she found it difficult to get into her jacket. He strolled across, his face a mask, and helped her, taking care, she was sure, not to touch her.

'I'm sorry,' she offered, her mouth dry, 'for withholding the payment you were obviously demanding for my meal. But, like you,' she faced him boldly, 'I've run out of the coinage, the currency necessary to oblige in that way. My—my emotional account doesn't balance any more. So I've closed it.'

His eyebrows arched over sub-zero eyes. The phone rang. He crossed the room and picked up the instrument as if he would have liked to hurl it through a window.

'Akerman.' He turned his back on Crystal. 'Lula?' He had not softened his tone. He listened. 'A job? This isn't a modelling agency, it's Worldview International you're speaking to.' His tone had a cutting edge that would surely have repelled the boldest of job-seekers. But not, it seemed, this one. 'Sorry, no vacancies.' His abrasiveness must at last have penetrated the skin of the caller, since a howl like that of a trapped animal rose into the room.

He listened some more, changing position slightly with an irritated jerk. 'You heard? OK,' with a sigh, 'so there might be something for you there. Look, I'm otherwise engaged. Maybe,' with a slicing glance towards Crystal, 'maybe not. No, the lady is decently clad.'

Now high-pitched, disbelieving laughter came over the phone.

'You know my office number, Lula,' he rasped. 'Ring there tomorrow. For old times' sake, give *you* a chance when the lady's gone?' Crystal could have sworn Brent ground his teeth. The phone clattering down was the caller's only answer.

It rang almost immediately. Lula trying her luck again, probably. 'Thanks.' Another crash of the receiver. 'Reception. Your transport's arrived.'

As he handed her into the taxi Crystal looked up at him. 'Thank you again——'

His dismissive shrug silenced her as effectively as he had silenced Lula.

Crystal's hand found its own way to the window handle. Her astonished eyes watched the glass slide down. Her astounded ears heard her lips pronounce the words, 'If you *have* to close down every branch of Ornamental You, couldn't you *please* spare mine? Maureen's got her invalid mother to care for. And I've got my rent to pay.'

As the taxi began to move she called back to the stiff, unyielding figure at the kerbside, '*Please*, Mr Akerman!'

For two weeks Crystal waited for the phone call that cold reason assured her would not come.

Every morning as she entered the shop she was met by Maureen's worried face. Every time she looked in the mirror she saw reflected back her own disappointment and unhappiness, caused, she informed her mirrored self, by the thought that in less than two weeks' time she would be without a job.

It had nothing to do, she told herself repeatedly, with the memory of what had happened between herself and Brent Akerman, nor with listening for his call, which was as likely to come as the moon leaving the sky and falling into the sea. Nor with the idea that she would never see him again, because a man scorned was probably just as furious as the proverbial woman scorned.

That evening the phone did ring. She stared at it, not believing her ears. Brent had relented; he had changed his mind, he liked her after all!

'Hi,' said Roger. 'Long time, yes, no?'

'Yes—no,' she echoed, unable for a few seconds to gather her madly disappointed wits.

'Two and a half weeks nearer to doomsday,' he quipped. 'Got another job yet?'

'No. Have you?'

'Nope. I'll be tackling my course work full-time. Hopefully, I'll be able to get a grant to cover my expenses. Er—about that little bit of help you were going to give me...?'

'I agreed, didn't I?'

'OK, so why so tetchy? I mean, if you want to change your mind...'

Crystal could almost see his shrug. 'No, I don't. And sorry if I'm irritable.'

'That's OK. Aren't we all at the moment, with most of us not knowing where our next stale crust is coming from?'

If only Roger knew, Crystal thought. Of course, she was worried about keeping a roof over her head, but that was not the cause of her short temper. It was raw, gnawing disappointment at the non-arrival of that call she was longing for.

'When do you want me to start?' she asked.

'How about this evening?'

'After tea? Or dinner or supper, or whatever's your word for it?'

'Grub,' Roger returned, laughing, 'just plain grub.'

He came on time, his small, somewhat battered car grinding to a halt at the kerb.

'Nice little nest you've got here,' he commented, glancing around the cosy living-room. 'Yours?'

'Rented.' She glanced at the pile of notes he was carrying. 'I hope you're not expecting me to finish all that this evening.'

'This? It's about three evenings' work, I'd judge.' He saw the computer on a desk in a corner of the living area and deposited his notes on the one clear corner. 'Have a look through them and see if you can decipher my scrawl.'

Crystal made a face at some of the corrections, but was able to work them out without Roger's assistance.

'Right, then.' He smiled from the door. 'I'll be off. I don't live that far from you, so I'll call in tomorrow, just in case you need a bit of help with my writing. That OK with you?'

Crystal nodded, secretly pleased that he was not intending to stay.

The follow evening he seemed to have other ideas. He staggered up the path, laden with folders and books.

'Not *more* work?' Crystal asked.

Roger shook his head. 'Thought I might do a bit of reading here, if you don't object?' He dropped his burden on to the sofa, then dropped himself on to it.

Don't sit there, Crystal wanted to cry, that's where I slept in Brent's arms...

'Well, I——' She frowned at the computer, then at him.

'I'll be quiet as a goldfish in a bowl,' he promised, his head persuasively on one side, 'honest.'

Crystal found herself laughing, even though she had wanted to say no.

'Good.' He settled more comfortably and hauled a heavy textbook towards him. 'Go ahead,' he added airily. 'I'm here,' with an engaging smile, 'if you—er—want me.'

She smiled, sensing the double meaning, but did not rise to his bait.

Twice during the evening she had to ask for an explanation. The second time, as he bent over her desk, he commented, sniffing the air around her, 'Nice perfume you use.'

'Do I?' She returned at once to her work, hoping she had diverted his attention from herself.

Partway through the evening he rose, stretched and asked, 'Got a kitchen in this oversized rabbit hutch?'

'No need to be insulting,' she returned good-humouredly. 'And the answer's yes.'

Deliberately misunderstanding, he was at her side in a stride. 'It is? Hey, Crystal,' he ran his fingers through his tousled hair, 'that's just great! Come on, into my arms.'

He tried to turn her, but she resisted. 'Don't be daft, Roger. Don't spoil our beautiful friendship. What's more, you'd be in danger of losing your secretarial help.'

His mouth turned down, then up. 'OK, so I'll bide my time.'

You won't, Crystal thought, but merely commented, 'I can take a hint. I'll put the kettle on.'

She had just finished the tray when the telephone rang. Thank heavens it's in the hall, she thought, noting with relief that Roger had turned on her television.

'Crystal? Brent here.' She couldn't get a word out for delight and a pounding heart. 'You OK? Or can't you hear me for background noise? Want to go and switch off your set?'

'N-no,' she answered, thinking that that was the last thing she wanted to do. 'I can hear you clearly.'

'Good. I've been abroad.'

'Surprise, surprise,' cracked from her parched throat as she tried her hand at a throw-away remark to hide her confusion at the sound of his voice after so long.

'Isn't it?' he remarked drily. 'Which explains why I haven't got in touch.'

Was the chief executive of Worldview International changing his mind after all? Was the company going to reverse its decision to close down Ornamental You?

'I see,' she croaked, her brain thrashing about for the right words. 'What about, Brent?'

'Hey, Crystal—— Oh, sorry,' Roger hissed in the background, 'thought your call had finished.'

She gestured madly behind her. 'Tea's made, tray's ready, could you——?'

'Right, will oblige.'

'You've got company?' Brent asked, voice studiedly neutral.

'Yes, a—a friend. But——'

'You should have told me. Goodnight, Crystal.'

Dismayed, she heard the click. He had gone. Now she would never know why he had called.

CHAPTER SIX

ROGER took it for granted that she wouldn't object to working at the weekend.

To Crystal's consternation, he had made a habit of bringing his work and staying for the evening. He had pleaded loneliness at his digs and she had not had the heart to ask him to leave his notes with her and go.

On Saturday evening he stretched and yawned. 'How about a break, pal? I've spotted a nice little pub near here—the Bull's Head. What's it like?'

Crystal's shoulder lifted and she continued with her work.

'Come on, partner!' He shook her shoulders. 'At this rate, you'll drop, and what good would that be to me?'

'You keep bringing the work,' she answered, giving in and going to tidy herself.

Over drinks in the Tudor-beamed inn, Roger commented with a crooked smile, 'Are you always this altruistic?'

'Come again?' Crystal responded, flicking hair from her ear and leaning towards him questioningly.

He laughed. 'Do you always work for no reward? What I mean is, since you started doing this work for me you haven't once raised the subject of payment.'

'Ah.' Crystal nodded. 'I've thought about it, though.' They laughed together. 'But I decided, in the circumstances, that, since you, like all of us, are going to lose your means of livelihood very soon, I'd postpone discussion of payment until you got yourself another job.'

'She is,' he pounded the table, 'she *is* altruistic—I knew it! In addition to having beauty and charm and sexiness.' He learned nearer. 'Any room in your life yet for a boyfriend, Crystal?'

She shook her head, her eyes looking inward to dwell on the face that lately had haunted her dreams. Since Brent's last call she had waited, again in vain, for a repeat. And the waiting was beginning to get to her.

Roger dwelt thoughtfully on the bubbles rising in his glass. 'That call the other night——' He glanced at Crystal, then down again. 'Kick me on the shins if you don't like me asking, but I thought I heard you say a name. Was it by any chance——?'

'Mr Akerman? Yes. And no, there's nothing between us, Roger.' How to explain her use of his first name? 'It's just that we've met—well, kind of unconventionally in recent times, and——' She hoped that her shrug reduced the apparent familiarity to a low level of significance.

'That's OK,' Roger responded, swirling the small amount of liquid in his glass as if he was seeking the right words. 'I was just wondering...well, at the meeting that night you stood up and spoke for all of us...'

'Wondering if,' she supplied, 'I had enough influence with Brent Akerman to appeal to him to alter his—or, rather, the company's—mind? I've tried it,' she wouldn't say where or how, 'but with nil result. Maureen was as disappointed as you are, not to mention me. And it's no use, Roger, asking me to try again.'

'I'll get us another round. Same again?' He looked no more cheerful on his return to the table.

'Roger——' he glanced up as she spoke, guardedly interested, as if his mind was elsewhere '—I haven't said it, but I've been thinking it all the time I've been working on your notes. I think you're really bright.'

He laughed loudly. 'All those chemical names, all that technical jargon? I must be blinding you with science.'

'No, honestly. I admit it's all beyond me, but I'm sure you're all set to get a good degree.'

'Thanks a lot. My ego's shining like the sun. And,' his hand touched hers under the table, 'I'd like to thank you for working so hard for my success.'

Crystal shifted her hand from his. She didn't want the conversation to become personal. 'It gives me something to do in the evenings. Keeps my mind off——' Brent, she thought '—off thoughts of the jobs I'll be chasing after soon. If I'm lucky, that is.'

Next day Roger announced cheerfully, 'I've brought sandwiches for two, plus liquid refreshment.' He unloaded his carrier-bag on to the kitchen table. 'Save you cooking lunch.'

Crystal shook her head, laughing. 'I could have used a tin-opener, and I've got canned drinks in the fridge.'

Roger made a face. 'My offerings sound like a feast against yours!'

Early evening, when they had eaten and cleared away the light meal that Crystal had cooked, there came a ring at the door.

Roger looked up from his studies. 'Visitors? Why didn't you tell me?'

Crystal frowned. 'I wasn't expecting any.' As she went to answer the second ring she glanced through the window. A long low car shone grandly at the kerb, making Roger's look fit for the breakers' yard.

It can't be, she thought, but it was. Brent Akerman stood on the doorstep, expecting to be invited in.

Brent swung round from the window, mouth a thin line. 'So Betts is granted the favours you chose to withhold from me.'

He must have seen Roger pretend to kiss her cheek, whispering in her ear instead, 'Who's an artful girl, then? No one but the top man will do for her, eh?'

He had moved away and she had had to reach out to his shoulders and pull him down to whisper, 'It's not like that, Roger. He—we aren't——'

'You aren't?' He smiled, then winked. 'OK, it's your business, but now's your chance to put in a good word for all of us. Right?'

He had left with a peck on her cheek and an encouraging wave.

'It might have looked like that to you,' she addressed Brent stiffly, 'but appearances are often deceptive.'

'Yes,' his hard eyes engraved a painful trail over her slender figure, 'they are, aren't they?'

She wished he had given her warning of his visit, she wished she had done her hair and dressed with more care. As it was, because she knew Roger wouldn't notice if she were wearing a sack tied with string, she had chosen to wear her oldest, most comfortable clothes.

Her blue blouse had shrunk and the buttons had to strain to do their work. Her jeans had fitted her well when she was seventeen, but that had been eight years ago... Instinct, however, told her that it was not her clothes he had been referring to.

'That's not true,' she declared warmly. 'I'm helping Roger out by typing his notes.' She gestured towards the pile of typewritten sheets on her desk, but Brent had not finished with her, nor listened, it seemed.

Hands in the pockets of his casual trousers, dark ribbed cotton sweater pulled over an open-necked shirt, he looked more human, yet at the same time more formidable, than she had ever seen him.

'You've discovered, have you,' he jeered, 'that you're not as emotionally bankrupt as you tried to make me believe you were? That there's enough coinage left in your erotic account, after all, to allow you to indulge in a casual affair? Or was Betts there in the background all the time, hence your mock coyness with me?'

The irony of it, she reflected helplessly. There's Roger, convinced I'm on more than friendly terms with Brent Akerman, and here's Brent, thinking I'm likewise with Roger!

'No to all your questions,' she answered. She twisted a button on her blouse, but stopped at once when his eyes dropped with very male interest to that part of her anatomy. 'If you think Roger was kissing me just now then think again. He was——' What was he? she floundered. Pleading with me to use my influence, such as it is, with you, and try to make you change your mind about the closures?

'Correct. He was. Chastely, for once, no doubt because he guessed I was watching.'

'No!' But how could she explain the unexplainable? So she lifted her shoulders and made to collect the empty cans. 'Think what you like, what you seem to *want* to think.'

She remembered her manners, that he was a guest in her house. 'I'm sorry.' She pushed her hands into her trouser pockets, once again catching his attention. His gaze dipped to her narrow hips, lifting to dwell on her small waist, rising yet again to linger on the rounded swell beneath the tight blouse. 'Why?' she went on, desperate to divert his attention from her body. His faintly lecherous looks were causing havoc to her feminine reflexes. 'Why did you come?'

He walked away, walked back, his perambulations taking no time at all, in view of the smallness of her living area. He stood in front of her, head high, glance slanted down, his hands, like hers, in his pockets. His proximity unnerved yet excited her beyond words. Did he know what he was doing to her? She had a shrewd idea that he did.

After a few moments of gazing at her mouth—even the movement of her lips seemed to arouse a sensual response in him—he walked away again.

Halfway back he said, 'I've been thinking things over.' He paused, deliberately tantalising her, she was sure.

'Yes?' she breathed, prompting him.

His smile was faint, as if he was enjoying himself.

Her large eyes sought his. 'Will you *please* tell me, Mr Akerman?' This was a side of him she just couldn't address by his first name.

His hand came out of his pocket and she thought he was going to touch her, but that hand merely smoothed back his slightly unruly hair. 'I've come to a decision. The board is with me on this.'

Her eyes lit up, her hands clasped tightly in front of her. 'You mean ... you're not—the company's not going to close down all the Ornamental Yous after all? Oh, Brent!' Her arms stretched out, wrapping round him, her feet went on tiptoe, bringing her within reach of his cheek. Her lips joined in the fun and placed a warm kiss there. 'Thank you, thank you so very much!'

Then she came to her senses and, colour high, released him, stepping back. 'Sorry,' she whispered, 'but it's such wonderful news that I couldn't——'

'What news, Miss Rose?' There was a familiar huskiness, the soft, intriguing tone she had heard at their first meeting. 'Shouldn't you wait until I tell you the company's decision before the gratitude pours from your——' his gaze dropped to them, then swung back '—lips?'

Her eyes clouded over; a frown pleated her usually smooth forehead. 'I'm sorry,' she said, disappointment making her voice heavy, her head turn away. 'Stupid of me to think there's ever any *good* news in this life.'

A hand beneath her chin turned her head back. 'So bitter, Miss Rose, so young? Is the break-up of your old affair still hurting?'

'What affair? Oh, you mean Mick——' She checked herself. She had as good as admitted that there had been more than close friendship between herself and her ex-boyfriend. Which there hadn't.

She waited now, her spirits as flat as a punctured balloon.

'The news,' he went on, releasing her, 'is not as bad as you might think.'

She looked up at him blankly, determined to keep a firm hold on her responses and her hopes.

'I put that last plea you made as you drove away the evening you dined with me to the board of directors of Worldview International.'

To her chagrin, he stopped. 'And?' she prompted, firmly quelling the hope that would keep springing inside her.

'And...' He smiled, then stopped.

'Tell me!' she cried, unable to stand his deliberate torment.

'And,' he relented at last, 'they've decided to allow one branch of Ornamental You to continue trading. The only proviso being that the takings continue to be as high as they have been in the recent past. For which,' his smile was a touch more genuine now, 'a prize was awarded, which a certain Miss Crystal Rose accepted on her branch's behalf.'

Crystal drew a deep, unbelieving breath.

'Now,' he went on, with his feet planted firmly apart, his arms folded, 'where is my reward for doing my best for the lady who has an invalid mother to look after, and for another, younger lady who has to pay her rent?' His eyes were a glinting challenge that would brook no refusal, no withholding of the reward he demanded.

'Oh, Brent,' she gazed up at him, eyes brimming, throat choked with emotion, 'thank you from the bottom of my heart. And Maureen's.' The tears spilt and she dashed them away with the back of her hand.

'That'll do,' he provoked, 'to be going on with. But it's not enough, Miss Rose, not *nearly* enough.' His voice had softened, which she had always found irresistible.

'Thank you, Mr Akerman—Brent,' she answered, moistening her dry lips. Her spontaneity, having once been checked, refused to function a second time. Only her eyes showed her gratitude.

He opened his arms wide. 'Well?'

She shook her head. 'Like you, I never mix business with——' Pleasure, she had almost said!

He saw her hesitation, guessed the reason and laughed, head back. A step towards her and she was swept into his arms. Lost in his kiss, she became aware that his hands were going on a voyage of discovery over and inside the over-washed blouse.

When she felt his hand moulding her breast she gasped against his mouth, stiffening instinctively and trying to draw away. It's wrong, a saner voice murmured, allowing him such liberties ... you know what he's after and you're not prepared to give, not without honest-to-goodness love ...

She felt him stiffen too, and began to count the cost of her rejection of him. Her withdrawal had seemed to anger him, and the kiss changed, his mouth becoming hard and merciless, invading and punishing, like his hands on her body.

As he put her from him at last his breathing steadied fast. 'Having got what you wanted from me,' he rasped, 'which is, I now see, what you've been after all along, you decide to call a halt?'

'It's not that, Brent——'

The insistent ring of the telephone cut across her halting explanation. Which was just as well, she thought, tucking in her blouse as she went to answer the call, since the 'explanation' was not one that she could possibly give voice to.

'Crystal Rose here,' she said through lips still aching from Brent's ruthless kiss.

Roger's voice came loud and clear. How could she stop it carrying to the man standing in the living-room doorway? 'How'd it go, Crystal?' Roger asked. 'Did you manage to charm you-know-who into a change of mind about the branch closures?'

'Roger,' she whispered hoarsely, 'he's still——'

'He is? For Pete's—— I'd better get off the line quick! Bye.'

The crash almost deafened her. It was not the one caused by Roger's speedy disconnection, but by the slam of the front door as Brent strode out.

Maureen was delighted when Crystal gave her the news, but Roger, when she had rung him back, had been deeply disappointed for himself and all the others, although good-naturedly pleased for her and Maureen.

'You'll carry on helping with my notes, won't you, Crystal?' he had asked.

'Of course,' she had assured him firmly.

'By the way,' he had added, 'the boss didn't hear me, did he?'

He had, Crystal knew, but she answered vaguely, 'Couldn't tell you. He didn't stay long enough for me to find out.'

'Thank God,' Roger breathed, ringing off.

Brent Akerman seemed to have faded from her life. Roger, on the other hand, began to figure in it more, sometimes, than she really wanted.

Custom at the shop continued steadily, even increasing a little, Maureen had calculated happily.

'It's been said before,' Roger commented when Crystal told him the good news, 'but I'll say it again. It's because of the bright smiles and welcoming manner of the two ladies who are running the place. Especially,' he reached out and patted Crystal's arm as she sat at the computer, 'this one. Don't you realise,' he added with a trace of wistfulness, 'just how much——?'

'Charm I've got,' Crystal broke in unsmilingly. Much good had that 'charm' done her where Brent was concerned! The days had lost their colour since his car had roared away from her house three or four weeks before.

'Crystal,' Roger stood beside her now, 'you and I,' his hand smoothed her hair, 'we'd make a good pair, yes? Did you know that the sun shining on these chestnut locks makes them gleam and glow? Sorry about the purple passage, but, well, it's what you do to a guy.'

She smiled up at him. 'Thanks a lot for the compliments, Roger.' She put her hand on his as it rested on her desk. 'But...'

'OK,' he sighed, returning to his seat, 'I'll wait. A broken heart does mend in the end, you know.'

Had he, she wondered with alarm, guessed her feelings for Brent Akerman? Then she realised he had been referring to the break with Mick, her ex-boyfriend.

Two days later Roger rang to say he wouldn't be coming that evening.

'That's OK, I've got plenty of your work to keep me going,' she assured him, then teased, 'Got a date?'

'Yeah. See you tomorrow.'

But two or three tomorrows went by before Crystal saw him again. When he did come back he seemed strangely pleased with life, and Crystal was happy for him.

'Anyone I know?' she asked casually.

'What? Who——? Oh, my date. Er—yes. Shirley Brownley. She said she saw you at the firm's dinner. Admired your hair colour, not to mention your looks.'

'I remember her. Blonde, full—er—figured.'

Roger laughed. 'You can say that again! She's OK. How're things at the shop?'

'Fine,' Crystal told him. 'Takings higher than ever.'

'Bet his lordship's pleased.'

'He doesn't know. I haven't seen him.' Nor heard him, Crystal reflected sadly, playing over in her head Brent's fine, low-pitched voice...soft and persuasive in her dreams, harsh and unforgiving in her daytime thoughts.

Arriving early a few days later, Crystal blinked hard as the morning sun reflected sharply off the shop's windows. She inserted the key, but found she could not open the door. Frowning, she studied the key, one of a bunch. Yes, she had been using the correct one.

She glanced at the windows. Of course it was the right shop! But those windows held nothing, not a single item. And the interior of the shop didn't look right, as though a wild animal had been let loose on its contents. Now she really began to be afraid, staring round for Maureen, wishing she would come.

She tried again, but the key was useless, so she put her shoulder to the door and it gave at last. She stepped in—and horror swamped her.

There was debris everywhere, glass smashed and splintered, shelving axed to pieces, metal fixtures torn from the walls, cardboard boxes empty, their contents scattered and broken. The shop's entire stock had been either destroyed or taken—the necklaces, the perfume testers, the toiletries...the shop had been thoroughly and remorselessly ransacked.

'Crystal!' There was a shriek from behind her. 'Oh, no, *Crystal*! Not us,' Maureen whispered brokenly, 'not our little shop. Whoever could have done this? Someone must really hate us, dear.' There was a sob in her voice.

Crystal, still stunned, shook her head. 'Routine robbery, I suspect. Not us, Maureen, the stock—they wanted the stock, not us.' She held her head. Brent Akerman, she thought, looking round for the telephone.

It was there, beneath a pile of rubble. 'It works,' she told Maureen, and dialled. She knew his office number by heart.

'Who——?' Maureen asked dully. 'Oh, yes, of course, the police.'

Shaking her head, Crystal listened. 'Would you put me through,' she requested as evenly as she could, 'to Mr Akerman's secretary, please? Oh, Miss—er——'

'Helen Cooper.'

'Miss Cooper. This is Crystal Rose, of Ornamental You. Could I speak to Mr Akerman, please?' Crystal wondered at her own calm tones.

'Sorry, Miss Rose, he's out of the office.'

'But I've got to speak to him.' Shock, she realised, was taking over. 'I *must*!'

'I'm sorry, Miss Rose, but—is it urgent? It is? Will you wait one moment, Miss Rose?' The phone seemed to go dead, then, 'I'm connecting you, Miss Rose.'

'What is it?' barked Brent.

Crystal was shaking now. It's only reaction, her reason tried to calm her. 'Something t-terrible's happened, Mr Akerman.' Her teeth were chattering now.

'Such as?' he enquired coldly.

'B-burglary, Mr Akerman. And they've really done their worst. They—they laid waste to it. They raided the till and the safe...took all the cash. And the takings were high, Mr Akerman. They've been so good lately. And now...' She drew in a sob. 'W-what shall we do?'

'How did they get in?'

'They got through a back window——'

There was a smothered curse, then, 'Told the police? No? Then do it, right now. Crystal? Are you OK? They didn't——?'

'It happened in the night, Mr Akerman. Maureen and I were at home.' Had she imagined that sigh of relief? But of course he would be relieved to hear about the safety of his employees, otherwise he might have had to pay compensation, mightn't he, or damages or something?

'Yes, I'm all right, Mr Akerman. I'm sh-shaking because I'm upset. And Maureen's crying.'

'Get the police there,' he insisted. 'Don't disturb anything until they've been.'

'No, Mr Akerman,' Crystal whispered, 'and I——' A sob escaped her.

There was a crash in her ear and he was gone. Even if he came, Crystal reasoned, the journey by car was a long one. Anyway, he hadn't said he would come.

'It's the end of our jobs, Crystal,' Maureen remarked unhappily. 'We've had a reprieve, that's all. Now we'll have to join the others in looking for work.'

The police arrived, and with them the questions. Crystal realised it was lunchtime, but she just wasn't hungry.

Maureen looked around hopelessly. 'Not much else we can do,' she commented, shaking her head. 'The place ought to be boarded up, but——'

'Anybody there?' A young man had emerged from a van at the kerb. 'Oh, hi.' He looked around. 'Mess, isn't it?' He smiled reassuringly. 'I've come to put the shutters up—you know, cover the windows and all that.'

Maureen managed a smile. 'You must have heard my thoughts,' she said. 'I was just saying——'

'Right, I'll get started. You ladies look as though you could do with a stiff drink.'

'Who sent you?' Crystal asked, frowning.

'Boss of the outfit contacted my boss.' Whistling, he went about his work.

When he had finished, Maureen pulled on her jacket. She looked around. 'Five years I was here. And this is how it had to end.' Bravely she stemmed the tears. 'That's it, Crystal. There's nothing we can do now until we hear from Head Office.'

Crystal was looking for her bag, finding it on one of the few glass shelves to have escaped destruction. 'I wonder who he meant, Maureen, by the "boss of the outfit"?'

'He meant me,' came a voice from the doorway.

Crystal swung round, half of her delighted to see Brent Akerman after so long, the other half dreading how he would take it. After all, it was partly their fault that the burglary had happened.

'Mr Akerman,' Maureen gasped. 'I never expected to see you here.'

'But how...? It isn't very long,' Crystal declared, consulting her watch, 'since I spoke to you at your office. How did you manage to get here so quickly?'

'Not at my office.' Brent walked in, crunching over broken glass in the semi-darkness. 'Helen called me up on my car phone, which is how I spoke to you. I'd stopped at a service station on the motorway.' He picked his way across the wasteland that had been an attractive, well stocked shop. 'The police—they've been?'

Crystal nodded.

'Right.' He took in the scene. 'I'll get things moving regarding clearance and so on.' He inspected the shutters. 'The place seems secure enough now.'

'We're sorry, Mr Akerman.'

He looked askance at Crystal. 'For what?'

She gestured towards the rear of the premises. 'For forgetting to close the window.'

'A burglary's a burglary,' was his throw-away remark, 'whichever way they got in.'

'It—it doesn't m-matter much to you, does it?' Crystal, to her horror, heard herself say. 'It's our livelihood, our means of earning to keep ourselves and——' motioning towards Maureen '—and our dependants.'

'Crystal!' Maureen chided, aghast at her colleague's outburst.

Brent's hard eyes had already stopped the verbal flow in its tracks. Crystal recalled his method of silencing her once before and coloured deeply, walking carefully to the door.

'I'm—I'm sorry. Thank you for coming, Mr Akerman,' she said, her voice still tremulous. 'And—and thank you from both of us for taking it so well.'

He inclined his head and followed them out, locking the door. 'For what it's worth,' he remarked with irony, pocketing the keys that Maureen had handed to him.

'Can I give you a lift?' His words were directed at Maureen.

'Thank you, Mr Akerman, but no. I only live five minutes' walk away. But Crystal——?'

'It doesn't matter,' Crystal answered, head high. He hadn't offered the lift to her, and she had her pride. 'A good walk will do me good. Bye, Maureen. Keep in touch, won't you?'

She started off in the opposite direction.

'Crystal!' The imperious command halted her along the street.

She turned. 'Yes?' Unable to resist, feeling his magnetism even in the depths of her despondency, she walked back, her expression carefully blank. 'You wanted to tell me something about the shop?'

'I'm taking you for a drink.'

'No, thanks. I wasn't included in the invitation——'

'Stop playing games.' His fingers closed round her wrist. 'You know damned well you were.'

They hadn't needed to drive there. It was across the road, the Wild Goose, a rambling, stone-built hostelry, with soft lighting illuminating the dining area. Brent had insisted on buying her a meal.

'You look pinched and agitated, Miss Rose.' His voice had softened. Did he know, she agonised, what a profound effect it had on her, that tone, that measured look? 'A good meal can do wonders for a system that's still in shock.'

She shook her head, fiddling with the cutlery. 'I don't feel like eating, thank you.'

All the same, when the meal was there in front of her she tackled it with a relish of which she was unaware until his chuckle brought her head up and she saw that her plate was almost empty.

He offered her the menu again. 'Thanks, but no second course.' She managed to smile. 'I really do mean it this time.'

'I'll take you home.'

'There's no need, thank you.'

He treated her refusal, she acknowledged with a blunt honesty, with the contempt it deserved.

As the car drew up outside her little home she felt bleak inside. How long before she saw him again? With the shop gone and her dismissal imminent, there need be no more communication between them.

His car phone rang, making her jump. He answered, looking at the time. 'Give me forty minutes,' he said.

No need, she thought, with relief mixed with disappointment, to ask him in.

'Thanks for the lunch,' she told him, managing a smile. She paused, her hand in the act of operating the door catch. 'That lovely crystal rose bowl that was awarded to our shop and which you presented to me—

I loved it.' She forced herself to swallow the lump in her throat. 'But it was somewhere on the shop floor, ground into little pieces, like all the rest.'

As she closed the car door she told herself she had been stupid even to mention it. Judging by the blank look on his face, he hadn't even remembered its existence.

CHAPTER SEVEN

'OK IF I come round this evening?' Roger asked on the phone three days later.

'Very OK,' Crystal answered with a sigh, relating the events that had led up to her extra leisure time.

'That's terrible,' Roger commented sympathetically. 'So all the stock was either destroyed or——'

'Taken. So I've plenty of time at home now to work on your notes. It's the only job I've got.'

'Join the club,' was his commiserating answer.

When he arrived he announced, 'I've brought the usual grub for us both.'

'We must take it in turns now,' Crystal prompted. 'Being both in the same financial boat, I mean.'

'We're not,' he answered, which statement moments later he seemed to regret. 'What I mean is——' He cleared a chair to sit on.

'You've got a private source of income?' she teased. 'I didn't know I'd been mixing socially with someone from the moneyed class. I must do a bit of name-dropping some time,' she added laughing. 'Roger Betts? Yes, a good friend of mine.'

'Don't be daft, Crystal. Maybe I'll tell you one day.'

'Don't bother,' she answered airily, seating herself at the computer. 'Your private business, especially the financial side of it, is just that. You should keep it that way.'

'Hm,' was his cryptic, if none too certain answer. 'How's Shirley?'

'Shirley? Oh, she's fine.' Roger smiled at his text-books. 'Nice girl.'

'I did guess,' Crystal responded, smiling.

'Not as nice as you, though.' His hand stroked the shiny cover of a particularly weighty volume.

Crystal's smile faded. She had hoped Roger had got over whatever feeling he might have had for her. 'Let's get down to it,' she stated, turning businesslike.

And get down to it they did. The kind of notes she watched appearing on the computer screen in front of her seemed to be getting more complicated, more scientific, going even more than usual right over her head.

It was no use asking Roger the reason, she decided, if reason did in fact exist, because she wouldn't understand his answer either!

Maureen called one morning. 'How are things?' she asked.

'Well, I'm getting nowhere, job-wise,' Crystal admitted despondently. 'What about you?'

'I've got a job,' Maureen confessed just a little hesitantly. 'Mr Akerman's found one for me—a clerical position in one of the firms owned by Worldview. I thought somehow,' she went on slowly, 'that he might have done something for you in that respect.'

Could her heart, Crystal wondered miserably, sink any lower? Brent obviously thought more of Maureen than he did of her. Those kisses they'd exchanged, his intimate caresses, sleeping in his arms—it had meant so much to her, but nothing at all to him.

'After he treated me to lunch the day of the burglary,' Crystal confided, 'I haven't seen anything of him. Never mind,' she was determinedly cheerful, 'it's just great that you've got work. I'm glad for you and your mother.'

Maureen hoped it wouldn't be long before Crystal was as lucky as she had been, and rang off.

That afternoon Crystal wandered aimlessly around the town, window-shopping, for the simple reason that she could not afford to do anything else. Returning home, she turned the key—and froze with fright.

Someone was in her house. Oh, no, she thought, not another burglary! For heaven's sake, what do I own that a thief would want? If she crept in she would catch him red-handed. Before her reason could tell her not to take such a foolish risk she held her breath, left the entrance door open and trod swiftly towards the living-room, where she sensed the burglar was.

The intruder, dark-suited, stood with his back to her, reading Roger's notes! Opening her mouth to scream, Crystal shut it quickly. That strong, straight back, those broad shoulders, the height of him—all of them personal features that had, over the past few weeks, become so familiar, and grown so dear to her.

Brent turned, plainly having heard her not so very silent approach, his smile mocking, until he saw her white face. Putting down the file he had been reading, he pushed his hands into his jacket pockets.

'If my being able to get into your house by unorthodox means has brought back bad memories,' he commented, 'then you must blame yourself.' At her puzzlement, he added, enunciating each word pointedly, 'You left a window open—at the back. A case of history repeating itself, yes?'

'But you're too—too solid to be able to squeeze through such a small opening.' How stupid that sounded, she thought, but his mere presence had sent her thought processes into their usual spin.

'My hand isn't.' He held it out. 'I pushed it through and turned the key in your back door. You should have bolts fitted for greater security.'

'I know I should,' she returned sharply—why did this man always have to catch her out?—'but I haven't got a handyman about the place to fix jobs like that.'

An eyebrow quirked. 'Fishing for volunteers?'

She coloured, admitting silently she had asked for that.

'I'd have thought,' he approached slowly, 'that Roger Betts would have obliged if you'd asked him nicely. He's always talking about you.'

'No, he isn't. He's got Shirley—Shirley Brownley. I'm not his girlfriend.'

'He seems to think you are.'

'I don't know why he——' She stared at him. 'How do you know all this? Have you given *him* a job?'

Brent just went on gazing at her. So he wasn't telling. She unshouldered her handbag and dropped the carrier-bag beside it.

'Been shopping?' he asked conversationally.

Something inside her reared up. He had helped Maureen and not her. And now it seemed likely that he had come to Roger's aid too, finding a position for him.

'How can I,' she heard her voice rising, expressing an anger that must have been simmering, without her conscious knowledge, ever since Maureen had imparted her news, 'go shopping when I haven't any money to spare because I haven't got a job? When I'm struggling to make ends meet, to pay my rent——'

'OK, OK,' he stood squarely in front of her, 'you've made your point. But let's get a proper perspective on things, shall we? Did *I* ransack the shop? Did I personally rob you of your livelihood?'

'Maybe you didn't,' her flushed face lifted to him, 'but...' She caught her breath. 'On the other hand, maybe you did. To get your own back, have your revenge.'

His teeth met with a frightening crack and he hauled her to her feet. His grip on her shoulders was so punishing that her head flopped as he shook her, once, twice.

'My own back for *what*? Revenge for *what*?'

His voice was a deep-throated growl. Crystal had never seen him so angry. All the same, she braved his anger again.

'Why aren't you honest,' she cried, 'and admit that you nurse a grievance against me? That because Maureen had to hurry home to her mother the other evening I was last out of the shop, which meant that it was my duty to lock the door, and you firmly believe I didn't lock it properly? It therefore follows,' she closed her mind to his darkening expression, 'that you're holding me responsible for the break-in. But you're wrong, because I *did* lock the door securely, I know I did!'

Brent let out an exasperated growl, his hands dropping to his sides.

'But,' she whispered, 'you won't believe me, will you, in order to give yourself yet another reason for overlooking me when it comes to handing out the compensating goodies in the way of jobs?'

He seemed puzzled, so she pressed on, operating the override button on her better judgement, 'You found a place in the company for Maureen Hilson, and it's obvious that you've provided Roger, too, with some kind of employment. Or——' Don't! her reason shouted, but she ignored its warning. 'Or was it because I said no that evening in your hotel room?'

'Have you quite finished?' His jaw thrust forward and he made a sharp movement in her direction. Instead he checked it, striding to the door.

Oh, God, she thought, he's going, and this time it will really be forever. How could I have said such terrible things to him, when I *like* him so?

'I'm—I'm sorry.' She ran after him and he turned. 'It's just that I——' Her voice dropped to a whisper. 'I've felt so—so low lately, so lost.' He took a slow step back into the living-room. 'I can't forget the sight of the shop when I walked away from it for the last time, the terrible mess, the destruction. I really loved working there.'

He stood, hands pocketed, regarding her. 'You're having a struggle financially?' She nodded. He indicated her desk, covered in printed sheets. 'I imagine your bank account's benefiting by quite a bit from what you're earning helping Betts.'

'Well, it isn't. I told Roger I'd wait for payment until he was in a better position financially.'

'So, a real labour of love,' he commented sarcastically, unmoved by the shake of her head.

Crystal rubbed her hand over the back of her neck and upward through her hair, shaking it around her shoulders. The movement attracted a narrowed look from him, but it relieved her own tension by a tiny fraction.

'Why did you come?' she asked, flopping down on to the sofa again. Then she remembered her role as hostess and stood quickly.

Quite plainly, she reflected, observing his aloof demeanour, it meant nothing that she had slept in his arms, because he most certainly hadn't come in the role of lover—*never* that—or even friend. Despite the casualness of his clothes, she judged that he had come on business. *Business*? she caught herself thinking with some bewilderment. How could he, when she wasn't his employee any more?

He wandered round the room, hands in jacket pockets. The busy street outside seemed to capture his attention. At last he said without preamble, 'I want a home, not a hotel room to go back to after a day's work. I've begun to like this part of the world. I've seen a house I'm thinking of buying, about six miles from here.' He turned. 'I'd value a woman's viewpoint about its location, its possibilities and so on. I'd be obliged if you'd agree to take on the role of female adviser.'

Crystal flopped down on to the sofa again, hostess role overtaken by astonished, somewhat flustered ex-employee.

'You want *me* to vet your prospective home? But why——?'

'Why not?'

An impossible, completely ridiculous thought had entered her mind, and her heart performed a kangaroo leap. Then she recalled his words...'take on the role of female adviser.' His tone had been impersonal and down-to-earth. I was right, she told herself, he has come on business after all.

'You really want to know what I think?' Crystal asked as they stood alone in the living-room of the house of his choice.

Brent commented, his lips faintly curved, 'I can read your opinion in your eyes. You like it.'

'Like it? It love it! It's a dream cottage.'

'So, as my female adviser, you'd recommend that I agree a purchase price and clinch the deal?'

Crystal frowned uncertainly. 'I speak as myself, not as or for any other woman.' Surely any female in Brent Akerman's life would hold very definite ideas on where she would, or would not, agree to live? 'Wouldn't it be better,' she added, although it almost killed her to speak the words, 'to bring the lady here?'

Ignoring her suggestion, he asked, 'The annexe—OK, so it's basically intended as living accommodation, but how would that grab you as office space?'

'For working at home on days when you don't need to go into Head Office? Just great. But that's only my opinion. Shouldn't you——?'

'No, I shouldn't, Miss Rose.' His tone held an edge that quietly told her it was none of her business whom he might bring there.

He watched her flush come and go, and she turned away abruptly, hating the way her body responded to him so readily, so warmly; hating him, too, for the ease with which he was able to manipulate her feelings.

A car braked in the tarmacadamed drive. Moments later a grey-haired man entered, apologising for having arrived too late to welcome her to his property.

'Charlie Western.' He extended his hand. 'It'll be a wrench leaving this place. Wayland Cottage.' He spoke the name as if he loved it. 'It's nearly three hundred years old,' he explained with a kind of sorry pride. 'I wouldn't be leaving it if I hadn't lost my dear wife.'

Short, trim-figured, he looked around fondly. 'I've enjoyed every minute we've—I've lived here, but I'm off to Canada to join my son and his family, so I'm leaving everything just as it is. Your young man here——' he smiled at Brent, then at Crystal, making her flush at his wrong assumption—Brent, *my young man*? she thought; he isn't even my *friend* '—says if he buys the cottage he'll buy the lot—furniture, fittings, even my car in the garage, and it's almost new.'

'Everything?' Crystal queried faintly.

Brent nodded, an eyebrow arching as if daring her to disagree.

Mr Western stared out into the wide, bright brilliance of the rear garden. 'Even the swing,' he added with sadness, 'that my wife and I bought for our grandchildren. But,' he brightened, 'I'll be living within daily reach of them over there across the Atlantic.'

Brent's bought the swing? Crystal thought, astonished. Had the woman who he'd claimed had soured him forever against commitment to the opposite sex come back into his life? And did she have a child old enough to enjoy playing on it?

Crystal tried to read the answer in Brent's expression, but it told her nothing. All the same, she was aware of her heart sinking out of sight.

'So what's the verdict?' They were back at Crystal's house and Brent was unzipping his jacket and hanging it on the coat-stand.

'As your female adviser?' Crystal attempted a bright smile. 'An excellent investment, I would say.'

'And as a woman?'

She shook her head. 'You didn't ask me to view it in that way.'

His eyes narrowed. 'Is Crystal Rose challenging me?'

'*Challenging* you?' Her smile was genuine this time. 'Never.'

'Provocation, Miss Rose,' his tone had softened even though the glint in his eyes was dangerous, 'will get you everywhere, even to places you never expected to go.'

Was it a promise? Or had it been a warning? She wished she knew the man well enough to know.

The atmosphere had acquired a tension that disturbed her, and she met the enigma in his eyes with a blank glance. Fencing with this man was something she found increasingly difficult to do. All she really wanted was to feel his arms around her again, to sink on to the sofa and——

'Would you like some coffee?' she asked, turning away and putting a sharp brake on her train of thoughts.

'Crystal?'

'Yes?' She turned to face him.

He held her shoulders, moulding them, and tiny electric shocks skittered up and down her spine. 'Relax,' he urged her down to the sofa, 'I'll get it.'

'But you don't——'

'I do. I found my way around this place the night I stayed here.'

With a resigned sigh she did as he had ordered. She had no other choice.

Brent disappeared into the kitchen, and there followed the rattle of crockery as the kettle sang, while over it all a melodious whistle rose. Crystal closed her eyes on the tears of thankfulness that had come from nowhere... he was there, quite plainly feeling at home—in *her* home.

Slowly the music his lips were producing registered on her conscious mind, a song with words from a distant century.

> There is a lady sweet and kind,
> Was never face so pleased my mind;
> I did but see her passing by...

And there he stopped. He hadn't completed the song; he had deliberately left the verse unfinished...

> And yet I love her till I die.

The tears of pleasure at his presence changed into tears of despair. She chided herself at her stupidity in thinking that such a man could ever *love* such a person as she, when he probably had a string of lady companions who would jump at his command at a mere ring of the telephone.

'Crystal?' He held the tray, frowning down at her. 'Something wrong?'

He had caught her dashing at her tears. Still annoyed with herself, she shook her head. He deposited the tray on a table and joined her on the sofa, lifting her chin and looking into her eyes.

'He hurt you that badly?'

'Who——? Oh, you're talking about Mick again.' She shook her head. 'It wasn't that——' But better by far, she told herself, he should believe that than guess at the real reason for the tears. She lifted careless shoulders. 'I was devastated at the time, but it'll pass. Or so they say.' Had her assumed nonchalance been convincing enough?

It seemed it had, since he nodded and arranged the cups to pour. He handed her one and absent-mindedly stirred his own, although he had refused her offer to fetch the sugar, which he said he hadn't been able to find.

He seemed preoccupied and, afraid to question him in case he gave voice to his thoughts, revealing them to be of the woman with whom he would be sharing the house he contemplated buying, she stayed silent, drinking her coffee.

'You remember,' he commented, 'the extension?'

So his mind was still on 'business'. Crystal didn't know whether to be pleased or disappointed. 'Built on to Wayland Cottage? Yes?'

He drained his cup and returned it to the tray, leaning back at last. The relaxed position of his body, however, did not seem to please his mind, and he got to his feet, which took him from one side of the small room to the other, then brought him to a stop in front of her.

'Roger Betts.'

The name, coming out of the blue, jolted her, arousing her antipathy. 'What about him?' Annoyed that he had put her on the defensive, she went on, 'We're friends, Mr Akerman. What's wrong with that? You've got no right to criticise me for working for him. You're not my employer now, so——'

His mocking smile stopped her. 'It goes with the colour of your hair.'

'What does?' She stood up, glowering at him.

'The temper. I merely said his name.' His smile faded. 'He must mean a lot to you if you go on the defensive about him when he hasn't even been attacked. The aforementioned Mick's been forgotten, then? In the space of——' he consulted his watch '——approximately twelve minutes.'

'I told you,' colour flamed in her cheeks, 'Roger and I——'

'Are just friends.' He nodded, plainly unconvinced. Hands pushed into waistband, he regarded her levelly, then walked away again. Crystal flopped back on to the sofa. She wished he would tell her what was on his mind.

He returned, hands pocketed.

'I repeat—Roger Betts.' He waited with amused eyes for another outbreak of irritation on her part, but she merely gazed up at him. 'He's working for the company again.'

Resentment welled, mixed in with jealousy and acute disappointment, all of which she managed to contain within her. She was pleased for Roger, of course she was, she argued silently, but why had she been left out in the cold?

'I guessed,' was all she said, staring up at him.

'And Shirley Brownley.' He paused, as if waiting for the explosion, and sure enough it came. She simply couldn't contain her disappointment any longer.

'Why?' she cried. 'Why not me too? What have I done, not just to go to the bottom of your list of potential employees, but to be struck off it? I need a job as much as they do...' Her voice tailed off, the backs of her hands pressing against her flaming cheeks. 'I'm sorry,' she whispered hoarsely. 'If—if I don't fit into your or Worldview's scheme of things, I quite understand.'

He crouched down and looked into her face, moving her hands from her cheeks. 'You understand, do you? I wonder, Crystal, just how much you do understand.'

She wanted to reach out and smooth back strands of his hair, touch his cheeks, press her finger against the resolute squareness of his jaw. She actually had to clench her fists and tuck them under her to stop them from taking such liberties.

'Not—not very much at all, really.' The admission came out as a whisper.

'So,' he straightened, 'maybe I'd better start at the beginning.' He moved away and she allowed her hands their freedom, rubbing their moistness against each other. 'One of Worldview's subsidiaries, name of Ornamental Cosmetics—you'll note that we've more or less retained the trading name—has come up with something brand new. A skin cream that cures blemishes and, the experts claim, keeps a lady's skin young-looking, plus, plus. You get me?'

Crystal nodded, still not daring to hope.

He stood at the window with his back to the light. Try as she might, Crystal could not see his expression.

'The product needs to be given a name and promoted.'

'Isn't it normal practice,' she remarked, feeling that at least one intelligent comment was called for here, 'to employ an advertising agency to do that?'

'Maybe that's what is normal practice, but refusing to follow convention can sometimes produce the best results. I'm getting a group together to do the job. I've already recruited two people. Betts—he already has a marketing background——' Crystal nodded, remembering Roger's experience at Head Office '—and Shirley Brownley. For a time she worked as a junior to the owner of a company selling advertising space.'

'Oh.' Crystal's heart took its familiar downward path.

'I need a third.'

'Oh?' Her heart began a slow climb up the hill again. 'There——' she moistened her lips. 'There should be plenty of people who'd be delighted to oblige.'

'It's not "plenty of people" I'm after. I'm fussy, Miss Rose,' his voice had assumed that seductive softness, but his face was as inscrutable as ever, 'and I want the one who's best suited for the job.'

'It goes without saying,' she agreed. 'But——' The clouds began to clear and an expanse of blue crept into her own particular piece of sky. There was even a glimpse of the sun, and she lifted slightly dazzled eyes to his. 'You don't mean——? No, you can't mean——'

'The winner of the prize for attaining the highest sales of the chain of shops known as Ornamental You?'

She shot to her feet. 'You're talking about *me*?'

'Can you think of any reason why I shouldn't be?'

'No, I... Oh, Brent—I mean, Mr Akerman, I——' All her impulses came together, urging her to fling herself at him as she had done the time he had told her that her particular shop had been spared from closure.

This time reason proved stronger and held her back. There was too much separating them now. He seemed to be in the process of turning himself into her boss again; he intended buying a cottage, probably installing a lady-friend there, even a wife... So she would have to restrain her instincts and make do with verbal gratitude.

'How can I thank you? I——'

'Surely you of all people know how?' His tone was seductive again, his eyes this time warm and teasing—and yes, he was challenging, daring her.

His arms opened wide. 'Crystal.' Huskiness was threaded through with a hint of command. Then she was in those arms, not sleeping this time, but very much awake, alive, in fact, in every throbbing pulse her body possessed.

When his lips met hers, and hers parted instinctively to accommodate his mouth, the truth struck her like a lightning flash... She didn't just like this man, she *loved* him, everything about him, the way his chest felt against hers, crushing hers mercilessly, the twisting muscles of his back beneath her arms as he pulled her down with him to the sofa and turned her to lie across his lap. The sweet cleanness of his breath, the thrust of his jaw as his lips' demands increased relentlessly.

And there was so much else about him that captivated her: the deep intelligence in his eyes, the authority in his tone of voice—yes, even his autocratic manner, which at times bordered on the arrogant, yet which, at other times, was transmuted into a softness that melted her limbs, robbing them of all resistance.

Now from deep inside her came a passion she did not even know she had, that must have lain dormant all through her friendship with Mick. When Brent's hands burrowed their way under her cotton top into which she'd changed before they'd gone out, when his palms found her breasts, stroking and moulding and with his fingertips finding their sensitised peaks, she was beyond the reach of her rational self and gave him all the ardent response that his lovemaking demanded from her.

His mouth was taking away the dryness of hers, slaking her thirst, yet increasing it so that she wanted more... and more of his intrusion. His hands were everywhere, unfastening her waistband now, pushing it down and skimming over the quivering surface of her stomach.

A passing car sounding its horn brought her back to reality, to everyday things, to a realisation that all Brent was seeking was a gratification of his needs, maybe even thinking of starting an affair...

For him it could be nothing more, because hadn't he told her that his emotions and his feelings were beyond repair? As hers would be if she allowed him in the heat of the moment to take from her all the warmth his body plainly craved in return, but which his steely resolve would prevent from even beginning to thaw that heart of ice, with which he claimed his past experiences with her own sex had left him.

He must have felt her withdrawal, the tension that stiffened her body within the circle of his arms. His hold on her slackened and she prised herself from him, getting to her feet as, with shaking hands, she put her clothes to rights.

'It seems,' she heard herself say with a sarcasm that was normally quite foreign to her, 'that you can't *give* anything to a woman without also *taking*.'

His expression told her nothing, but, as she stared at him, it was the cold fire in his eyes that brought a shiver to her overheated flesh.

His arms were outspread along the sofa's upholstered back, and his shirt, opened to the waist, revealed the mat of hair which, only moments ago, her face had been burrowing against, and which was now drawing her back like a powerful magnet. Head back, eyes flashing, she fought against its pull.

'Thank you for your offer of employment Mr Akerman, but——' how could she, she asked herself, how *could* her pride make her throw back in his face the job she so badly needed, that she *wanted* so much? '—but I'm not prepared to p-pay the p-price you're demanding in return.' Her emotions were tearing her assumed composure to pieces, but she would keep her dignity, she vowed, even if it killed her.

His eyes had turned glacier-cold. His jaw thrust forward, then he was on his feet in one swift movement, rebuttoning his shirt.

'Don't you mean, Miss Rose,' he gritted, 'that it isn't only your *emotional* account that's empty, it's also the material one that you have with your bank. Plus, you suddenly remembered that you already have a lover, and, since he owes you so much cash for the work you've done for him, you decided you'd better stay faithful to him until *that* payment is forthcoming, solving your personal cash-flow problems. Then,' he was jerking on his jacket now, 'you might—just—consider indulging in a parallel affair? If so, *Miss Rose*,' he added bitingly from the doorway, 'count me out. I like any woman I might take a fancy to to be unattached in mind *and* body in the short period of time they share my life, and my bed.'

'Hi, Crystal,' said Roger over the phone one evening a week later, 'congratulate me. I've got me a job!'

'That's great!' Crystal exclaimed. How, she wondered, had she managed to sound so surprised? She could have told him, 'I know.'

'Which means,' he went on, 'I can pay you the money I owe you for all that work.'

'That's great too,' she answered with a laugh. 'Don't I need it!'

'You do?' There was a thread of genuine surprise running through his tone. 'Well, if that's so, why...?' He had plainly decided not to finish the question. 'OK, I'll be round to settle my debts straight away. Er— Shirley's got a job too.'

'She has?' I knew that as well, Crystal thought. 'Good for Shirley! And Maureen Hilson told me she's been lucky.'

'Yeah, but——' Here comes the question, Crystal thought, that he'd thought better of asking just now. 'What about you, Crystal? I heard rumours that the big boss himself had one lined up for you.'

'You did?' Again the simulated surprise, but she couldn't stop herself from sighing, unable to keep up the pretence. 'Roger, I did a silly thing. I——'

'Hold it,' Roger cut in. 'I'll be round in fifteen minutes flat. I've got a nice solid shoulder for you to cry on. Hadn't you noticed?'

He kept his word, arriving on time, cheque at the ready. 'This should keep the wolf from the door for a month or two. There's more—work, I mean.' He lowered a fat folder to her desk in the corner of the room. 'Can do? Since you haven't got a job after all, I mean?'

'Can do, Roger.' She sank into a fireside chair, gripping the wooden arms. 'That silly thing I did—no, I can't burden you with my idiotic ways.'

He took one white-knuckled hand in his. 'Spit it out, pal. This,' he patted his shoulder, 'is ready and waiting.'

Crystal looked up at him, and without a warning her eyes filled. 'That job—I turned it down. Wasn't I mad?'

Roger stared. 'Mad? You must have been totally and completely crazy! For Pete's sake, why?'

She shook her head, unable to speak. The phone rang and Roger lifted a fist as if to hit it. He looked at Crystal, who was busy searching for and finding a handkerchief, so he leaned over and lifted the receiver.

'Who's that, and what do you want?' he snapped into it, uncharacteristically impolite, seeming strangely upset by Crystal's tears. 'Yeah, she's here, but who——?'

Crystal, getting to her feet, hardly daring to hope, took over the call, her hand shaking. 'Y-yes?' she asked, but the caller, whoever it had been, had gone.

'Know who it sounded like?' commented Roger wonderingly.

'Mr—Mr Akerman?'

'Yeah, Mr A in person, I'd guess.' As Crystal's tears turned to sobs he frowned in sympathy and patted his shoulder. It was a comfort of the brotherly variety, and Crystal used it thankfully. Drawing away at last, she apologised for the dampness she'd left behind, but he dismissed this with a wave.

'Any time. Now spill the beans. Come on,' he reached into the carrier-bag he had brought and produced a couple of cans, 'drink while you talk. They're not alcoholic, but the fizz in 'em 'll put the fizz back into you. Yes?'

She had to smile, scrubbing at her damp cheeks and taking a drink. She couldn't possibly tell Roger the truth about what had happened between Brent and herself.

'I—well, I just didn't like the sound of it,' she invented lamely, putting the partly consumed drink aside. She hadn't even known what the job would have consisted of.

'Didn't like the sound of it?' Roger repeated, aghast. 'Hell, Crystal, it was a job of jobs! Not to mention the kudos that went with it.'

Crystal shook her head, then shrugged. She wished she understood what Roger was talking about. It was plain that he knew a great deal more than she did.

'What's the use of telling me that now?' she said faintly. 'The opportunity's gone. They say it hardly ever knocks twice, so——' Another shrug. 'Anyway, thanks, Roger, for increasing my almost non-existent bank account.' She managed a smile. 'And for the work.' She gestured to the folder. 'I'll get started right now.'

'Fine.' He smiled back. 'Right, I'll be on my way, Crystal.'

She smiled. 'Thanks for the loan of the manly shoulder.'

He smiled back. 'All part of the service.' He drained his can, dropped a kiss on her surprised lips and left with a wave.

Sorting idly through the highly technical handwritten notes that Roger had left, Crystal wondered if the caller really had been Brent. If so, why had he phoned? And why had he rung off as soon as she had answered? Well, she would never know now, would she? she reflected with a sigh.

Two days later the postman delivered a letter that sent her heart into a spin. It came, it seemed, from the secretary to the chief executive of Worldview International. The letter ran,

Dear Miss Rose, I am writing to inform you that you are invited to attend an interview at Head Office, connected with the possible offer of a position within Ornamental Cosmetics, a newly created subsidiary of Worldview International.

The date and time of the interview was stated, and the interviewee was requested to signify in writing her acceptance or refusal of the above-mentioned appointment.

Overjoyed, Crystal threw her arms high, then, in the absence of any available human being, dived for a cushion and hugged it to her. Had Brent relented and decided, in spite of her impulsive and, she had to admit, foolish rejection of his initial offer, to give her another chance? If so, why? And had that been the reason for his phone call the other day when Roger had answered?

Maybe—she hugged the cushion anew—opportunity did knock twice, after all!

CHAPTER EIGHT

THE interview area was furnished with two-seater settees arranged in a wide circle. Each occupant had his or her own adjustable table on which to write notes. The room had plainly been designed so as neither to intimidate nor overawe, but overawed Crystal certainly was.

The interviewing committee consisted of six people, two, she noted, being female. One male—very male—committee member overawed her very much indeed. Central to the group and the sole occupant of his particular settee, Brent reclined, arms outspread along its back, his suit jacket opened wide.

The position reminded Crystal—the memory, threatening her poise, stole up on her unawares—of the last time he had been in her house, when she had torn herself from those arms of his and had thrown his offer of employment back in his face.

'Right, Miss Rose,' he clipped, having introduced her with cool politeness to the assembled company, 'sell yourself—to the committee,' his eyes half closed, looking her over as if he, too, was back in that time when, her clothes in disarray, she had lain so willingly in his arms, 'but, most of all, to me.'

There was a harsh ring to his voice, not a trace of the softness with which, in the past, he had spoken her name. He was angry with her? Because Roger had been with her the evening he had phoned her, then cut the call? So why had he changed his mind and given her another chance? Not, she told her swiftly hopeful self, because of any change of heart on his part—hadn't he warned

her that that heart of his would never again warm up
for any female of the species?

Eyes diamond-hard, mouth set in a formidable line,
he regarded her unwaveringly. Challenge issued from
every part of him; and to Crystal he was the most
daunting object in that room. Well, she informed herself
defiantly, it was a challenge she would rise to!

'Please sit down, Miss Rose,' an understanding voice
invited. She looked gratefully towards the white-haired
lady speaker and lowered herself into the only single
armchair in the room. Crossing her legs and arranging
her skirt to give her hands something to do, she grew
conscious of the more than interested regard of the
chairman of the committee.

About to shoot him an angry glance, she remembered
where she was and called her wayward reactions to heel.

'Go on, Miss Rose.' His tone was softer now, but with
a goading kind of edge to it.

'Can we——' she moistened her lips '—can we start
at the beginning, please? I—um——' Was she being
audacious, was she in the act of crossing her own name
off the short list? She decided that now she'd started,
she might as well go on. 'I received a letter inviting me
to this interview. It didn't contain any information about
the work being offered, but I was——' she glanced
around, hoping for a sympathetic hearing '—I needed
a job so much that I came here on the strength of that
letter. So if you could tell me—I mean, if I could be
provided with a job description...?'

There was general laughter, and Crystal smiled with
relief, a little of the tension ebbing out of her.

'Well said, Miss Rose,' Brent commented lazily. 'Point
to you.' He actually leaned forward and made a mark
on a sheet of paper. So he had intended to faze her,
throwing her in at the deep end? 'Helen?' He half turned
to a young woman seated a short distance behind him.

Slim and attractive, Brent's secretary stood, and Crystal noted in passing that she wore a wedding-ring. Why that fact should be so reassuring to her, Crystal could not imagine.

'There is a vacancy, Miss Rose,' Helen Cooper addressed Crystal personally, 'in the small company that has just been formed under the auspices of Worldview. This new company's name is Ornamental Cosmetics.'

That much at least, Crystal thought, I know.

Helen smiled at Crystal, then continued reading from a printed sheet.

'Its first product,' she pronounced, 'is a skin cream whose formula remains, and will continue to remain, a strict secret. Its name has to be decided and approved. The product needs to be launched, with appropriate hype, on to the cosmetics scene, then promoted and marketed.'

The secretary turned a page. 'The person appointed to the vacancy for which you are now being interviewed would become one of a team of three. The committee would be interested to read your curriculum vitae and to hear your views as to why you consider yourself qualified to become one of the team.'

The secretary resumed her seat.

Curriculum vitae? Crystal's reproachful gaze swung to Brent. Why hadn't he told her? She hadn't brought it.

'Well, I——' She had to gather her wits and, in the absence of written evidence, make a case for herself! 'I worked for Worldview—Ornamental You, that is—for nearly a year, until I—until the shop was——' She looked at Brent for help, but he was plainly determined to give none, so she ploughed on. 'Before that I was employed by my uncle in the marketing company he owned.'

'What exactly was your job within that company?' Brent asked, although Crystal reckoned that he must

have known the answer from her personal file. Was he
trying to help her after all?

'Well, my uncle was determined, he said, to make sure
that I learned the trade, as he called it, by tackling a
variety of jobs.'

One of the men nodded in encouragement.

'For instance, he put me on to analysing the results
of consumer research. I learnt about the lifestyles of potential consumers, their needs, their spending inclina-
tions, their tendency to self-denial where their needs were
concerned when set against the needs of their families.'

'Very interesting,' said one of the ladies.

'And why did you leave that job, Miss Rose?' one of
the men enquired.

'I'd joined the firm straight from school. When my
uncle retired I thought it was time I extended my knowledge of marketing by moving into the retail side of the
business. In other words, I wanted to make *personal*
contact with consumers.'

'So you applied for a job with the Ornamental You
chain?'

Crystal nodded.

The question came from Brent.

'Yes,' she answered unequivocally. 'I liked coming into
contact with ordinary people. I enjoyed it so much while
it lasted.'

The committee members nodded sympathetically.

'We've heard quite a lot about you,' the sympathetic
lady told her. 'The chief executive,' she added in an encouraging tone, 'has already made a strong case in your
favour.'

Crystal's head turned sharply to the man in question.
Why? His mind didn't even seem to be on her. He was
doodling around the margin of his notes. She was,
however, given the answer—the plain, down-to-earth,

unsentimental answer, by another member of the committee.

'He told us that you and your colleague,' interpolated a young to middle-aged man, 'collected the prize for the highest sales of stores comprising the now defunct chain of Ornamental You.'

'That even when the rest of the chain was closed,' said another, older man, 'yours went merrily on, gaining even more custom and clocking up even higher sales.'

'Thank you for——'

'The sales talk,' Brent pointed out a little too smoothly, 'this *personal* sales talk, Miss Rose, should have come from you.'

'Implying,' Crystal could not prevent herself from retorting, 'that if I can't *sell* myself I wouldn't be able to sell the new product in question?'

Eyebrows lifted, Brent continued doodling as if he knew the fiery ways of the lady interviewee's temper, and breaths were expelled in relief at his lack of response.

'I'm sorry, Mr Akerman.' She clutched her bag and started to rise.

'Oh, dear,' said the white-haired lady, 'this young woman seems determined to walk out on this interview. Well, I think we might by now have all made up our minds?' There was general assent. 'So,' she glanced around, 'I think we should put her out of her misery and let her go. Agreed, Mr Chairman, ladies, gentlemen?'

The chairman seemed to be silently cursing his unexpectedly broken pencil, but the committee nodded, and the secretary politely showed her out.

'Would you mind waiting in my office?' Helen said.

Crystal looked around. 'Where are the other applicants for the job?'

'They were all interviewed last week,' Helen answered. 'You were the last. OK?' With a smile she returned to the others.

The discussion percolated through to Crystal as a mere murmur of voices. The committee, she hazarded, must have made up their minds before her interview, and she had been called simply out of consideration for her enhanced status as a prize-winning ex-employee of Worldview. Or had it been Brent's conscience that had moved him to invite her there, having found jobs for the others?

Ten minutes later she was being shown back into the interview-room. She braced herself. The jury no doubt had found against her.

To her astonishment, only Brent was present, behind a desk which earlier she had not noticed. He called her across the room, having dismissed his secretary.

He gestured, inviting her to take the seat not at the other side of the desk but at an angle to his swivel chair. His head was turned from her and she tried to read his profile. She could see no signs of encouragement, and this upset her immoderately. It could only mean that she had failed to get the job.

'You didn't give me a chance,' she burst out. 'Sending me that letter out of the blue. I didn't even know what the interview was about. If I had I'd have updated my c.v., brought it with me——'

'You've got the job.'

'I'd have... Excuse me, but what did you say?'

He swung to face her and she felt the full impact of his presence, his strong features set into an unreadable mask, his tough physique, his top-to-toe pulling power.

'You've got the job. If you want it.'

'If—if I *want* it? Oh, B——' She had so nearly overstepped the mark! How could she almost have let herself take the liberty of calling *this* man by his first name? 'I'm so h-happy! Of course I want it. I——'

Unable because of protocol and all the other inhibiting factors to express her pleasure in her customary fashion, she found the only other way round the problem. The tears welled and spilled over with the sobs that shook her.

When a large folded handkerchief was pushed into her hands she pressed it against her cheeks, her eyes, her mouth. It held the now too familiar scent of him and she never wanted to let it go.

'S-sorry,' she mumbled, calmer now. 'What can I say but—thank you?' She handed the handkerchief back, then saw how her eye make-up and lipstick had left their mark on the shining whiteness. 'Please, let me take it home and wash it.'

His only response was to push it into his pocket, his eyes holding a message she longed in vain to decipher. A smile lurked, too, reminiscent, reflective. The air was filled with unuttered words, thoughts clamouring to be spoken out loud...

'How——' she cleared her strangely hoarse throat '—how did it happen? Those other applicants—was I *really* better than they were, or——?'

'Did I manoeuvre and manipulate the committee into taking the decision to choose you? On what grounds would I do that?' His eyebrows rose autocratically, and just a little reducingly.

It was, she thought, as if there had never been anything between them, as if she'd never slept snuggled up to his chest, never felt his hands on her body, never succumbed to his caresses and his kisses.

'I assure you, the decision to choose you was fair and above board.' Brent swung minutely from side to side in the swivel chair, regarding her narrowly. 'We knew about your previous experience. It's in your personal file. The committee obviously wanted to interview you as they interviewed the other candidates, before coming to their final decision.'

'Of course,' she whispered, feeling smaller than the tiny crystal bird that perched on its stand on a corner of his desk. 'Of course they did,' more emphatically.

Somehow she had to save face, to clear from his mind the suspicion that she had thought he might have promoted her interests because he... because they...

'For such an important post,' she added, 'an estimate of potential based on personality plus experience would be absolutely necessary.'

'You're so right,' he commented drily.

'I——' Crystal looked down at her hands, which of their own accord were clasping and unclasping '—I honestly thought that the fact that I didn't bring my curriculum vitae would ditch my chances.'

'In view of what I've just said, it didn't matter. You'd been an employee—a successful one—of the company. That counted more than anything.'

The interview seemed to be at an end. She stood up, her legs still somewhat unsteady at her sudden acquisition of a job, not to mention the fact that very soon she would be able to live above the poverty line again, paying her rent on time, not to mention all the other bills that lay in wait like an animal about to pounce and gobble her up.

'Don't you want to know,' he asked, brow lifting quizzically, 'how much your salary will be? Also, when your new job starts? Not to mention the names of the other members of the group you'll be working with?'

Another gaffe, she reproached herself. Of course she should have asked those vital questions.

She sank down again. 'Yes, please.'

'There'll be the three of you—Betts, Shirley Brownley and you. You know what will be required of you?'

'You've already explained. The day you——'

'You turned the job down?' he interrupted briskly. 'Well, now you've got it. And accepted it this time, I hope?'

'Accepted with pleasure, Mr Akerman.'

'Fine.' He proceeded to name a sum that brought a gasp to her throat and caused her to flop back into the chair. He leaned forward, threat in his eyes, and something else that made her body tingle. 'And if you dare to tell me you're not worth that——' He was interrupted by the buzz of the intercom. 'Yes?' sharply. 'OK, OK.' He glanced at his watch, about to switch off, then added, 'Thanks, Helen, for reminding me. I'm due at the airport,' he told Crystal, 'in one hour. In a few days you'll be receiving the appropriate contract, plus job specification and so on.'

Another glance at his watch had him piling papers together, searching in drawers for folders that didn't seem to be there, and pushing his pen into his pocket.

'By the way,' his eyes had already taken on a far-away look, as if in his imagination he had propelled himself into the foreign places towards which he was about to fly, 'a condition of the job offer is that, prior to starting work, you, along with the other two, attend a three-week intensive course covering the whole area of product marketing and related subjects. This should help to consolidate the experience the three of you have already had in that field. They've agreed. Do you?'

'I agree,' she answered promptly. 'Naturally I agree.'

'Naturally,' he echoed satirically, and the flash in his eyes of the Brent she knew and loved made her heart leap, but the businessman side of him made it crash helplessly to earth. 'Your place of work will be the extension to Wayland Cottage, which is now legally mine,' he said. 'I've had it converted and equipped. Remember?'

How could I forget? Crystal wanted to say, but merely nodded.

'What will you do for transport?' he asked.

'You mean, how will I get there from my house? Buy a bike,' she answered promptly.

'On the salary you'll be earning? Why not a car? I know you can drive.'

She shook her head firmly. 'Not a car, thanks—a bicycle. I like the exhilaration of the wind in my face and the high I reach sometimes when I'm exercising. Better for my health, better for the environment...'

'OK,' with a smile that made her heart jump again, 'you've made your point.'

She got to her feet, finding her legs just a little unsteady. 'Are you,' she ventured, 'going abroad again?' She heard the trace of disappointment and hoped he had not.

He stood up. 'I am.'

'Oh. Where to this time?' The way she had phrased the question must have given away to him that she still had not forgotten their first meeting, or their second, or their...

'The Bahamas, then South America.' There was the flash of smile over his expressive mouth. Had he remembered after all? 'Would you like to come with me, Miss Rose?' The softness—it was back!

She knew he hadn't meant it. 'I... Chance would be a fine thing, Mr Akerman. How——' she had to clear her throat '—how could I take leave of absence, for instance, from a job I haven't even started yet?'

One or two steps brought him close enough for her to feel the brush of his breath on her mouth. 'You could, with the boss's permission.'

She shook her head, hoping her heart wasn't in her eyes. Her lips parted to say that it was impossible, when his hands curved over her shoulders and she was impelled slowly towards him. His mouth touched hers, lingered, lifted, touched again. '*Au revoir*, Miss Rose,' that mouth murmured against hers. Then she was free.

A few more seconds in which his quickened breathing slowed itself down, then his manner returned to normal. Wide strides took him to the door, and he waited to see her out.

'Thank you, Mr Akerman.'

Those eyebrows shot up. 'Never thank a man, Miss Rose,' softly, 'for a kiss *you* allowed *him* to take.'

The implication stung that the invitation had come from her. 'No, no, I meant for the job. For—everything.'

'Any time.' His handshake was more of a caress than a dismissal.

If he noticed that her smile was tremulous, she didn't much care. He would think she had been moved to tears by the sudden upward turn in her fortunes. Never in a million sunrises would he guess the real reason—that, despite that kiss, it was the thought of never again being on friendly, let alone more than friendly, terms with him that was upsetting her so.

Brent must have moved with the speed of light, Crystal decided as she looked about her. So much had happened to Wayland Cottage since he had shown her round that she could hardly believe her eyes.

New carpets had replaced worn ones, the décor had been recently finished, judging by the aroma that teased the nostrils, while new curtains hung instead of those left behind which had not matched the new shades, plus all the other alterations and improvements.

The letter she had received along with the contract had requested her to attend at the country residence of Mr Brent Akerman. Would she then, the letter instructed, collect the keys to the suite of offices from Mrs Mary Carlyle, the newly installed housekeeper?

'I was told to expect you,' that lady remarked, inviting Crystal in. Brown-haired, carriage upright, she added with a smile, 'And may I say that you're every bit as pretty as I've been led to believe.'

Leading Crystal into the living area, she did not see the high colour that her words had caused. So who'd been talking? Crystal wondered, eyes bright with hope. Then they dimmed as she told herself severely to be sensible. It couldn't have been Brent. He was abroad. So it must have been Roger.

'You're the first,' Mrs Carlyle informed her. So it hadn't been Roger. Well, the problem—if problem it was—would remain unsolved. 'Now, I've been told to feed you all at the appropriate times—morning coffee, lunch for the three of you, afternoon tea, even evening meal if that's what any of you want. He's a good employer, is Mr Akerman.'

Crystal, having learnt by past experience, could not but agree.

Money had been spent as freely on equipping the offices as it had on the cottage. Technology reigned supreme, new ways and equipment were everywhere, all of which Crystal found just a little daunting.

Besides the larger office, where she assumed she and the others were to work, there was a smaller office near the entrance which, when she tried the door, proved to be locked. By the larger than average desk and the comfortable furnishings, she judged it to be reserved for the owner himself.

The others, when they arrived, expressed their pleasure at their working environment, not to mention their surprise. And not a small amount of apprehension.

'He certainly expects results, does our Mr Akerman,' commented Shirley, swinging round on an office chair, 'judging by all this hi-tech stuff. I'm glad that it,' waving towards the shining new equipment, 'was part of the course curriculum, otherwise just looking at it would have scared me silly!'

'Right, so come on, all of you,' prompted Roger, 'let's get down to business. Every second, when you're on trial, counts. And don't let's fool ourselves, girls—we are on trial. And,' he looked as serious as he sounded, 'there's another thing. It's occurred to me that this group—us—has been assembled as a kind of job-creation scheme.'

'You mean, to give us work as a way of salving their consciences for sacking us?' Shirley asked, frowning.

'Possibly, yes. Whether we're really subsidised by Worldview, or by a guy called Brent Akerman personally, I wouldn't know—— Whatever,' Roger shrugged, 'we've *got* to give him, or them, their money's worth. Lecture over. So, let's give it a go, shall we?'

As the days passed they were faced with problems they did their level best to solve, such as the shape of the jar that would hold the precious substance it was their job to promote, and the colour and design of the labels that would touch the womanly instinct and make a lady select their particular product.

In the end they sought and found outside help, and the design the artists finally came up with was, in the opinion of all three, both practical and pleasing to the eye.

The name proved even more difficult. 'Come on, you two,' Roger urged, 'this is something we've got to produce from inside ourselves. No outsider can help us here.'

'Cream So Soft?' Shirley suggested, stroking her cheeks. 'It's worked wonders on my spots.'

'Spot Squasher?' teased Roger, to laughter.

'Smooth as Silk,' Crystal offered, at which once again they shook their heads.

Three weeks into the project, when Shirley had left for home and Crystal was preparing to do likewise, Roger announced that he was off to visit the laboratory.

'Ornamental's?' Crystal asked with a smile.

'Who else's? I thought that seeing a real live lab—a commercially based one—might help me with the practical side of my course. I've got to know one or two of the chemists who work there, so I thought that if I wore this,' he indicated the Ornamental name tag pinned to his jacket, 'they might lower the mental drawbridge and let me through the security net.'

'I suppose it's worth a try,' Crystal conceded, 'just as long as they don't misunderstand your motives. Especially if it's going to help you with your studies.'

'It'll be great to get the feel of the place, of the working environment, if nothing else.'

Crystal was resting exhausted on her sofa at home a few days later when the telephone rang. Reaching out for it, she said wearily, 'Roger, you know how tired I am——'

She caught her breath, her skin tingling. She knew, she *knew* who was calling, although he had not spoken a word. He had been in her thoughts day and night since he had gone. How could she be sure she wasn't still dreaming?

'*Brent*?' she exclaimed. 'I'm sorry, I mean, Mr——'

'What's wrong with "Brent"? And how did you know when I hadn't even identified myself? Don't tell me, it was that intuition of yours. And why are you so tired?'

'I'm t-tired because we've all been w-working hard.' Pleasure and disbelief that Brent had called her from across the world was ruining her composure.

A pause, then, 'So how's the project going?'

He wanted a factual report on their progress? So it was a business call after all. She cleared her throat and all sentiment from her thoughts.

'We've made a lot of contacts,' she reported, her tone matching his in its 'this is business' tone. 'We've worked on the design of the jar with the help of a group of artists Shirley knows, contacted a marketing company, paid for their advice regarding product promotion, market research, costing and pricing, not to mention media advertising. Are we,' she dared with a smile, 'earning our keep Mr Akerman?'

'Repeat after me: Brent.' She did. A few breathless seconds went by. 'And yes, the venture capital with which the parent company is backing the three of you,' so, Crystal thought, I guessed right, 'to launch their cherished new product seems to be in good, hard-working hands. No wonder you're tired! Are you,' with that unnerving softness, 'sitting down?'

'I—er—think it's called reclining.'

'Oh. On which piece of furniture?'

'The sofa.' A long pause this time.

Was he remembering? 'Ah. Yes.' He was.

'Where—where are you calling from?'

'The south of France.'

'But I thought you were going to South——'

'I did. I've been forward in time, backward in time. I'm . . . tired too, Miss Rose.' There it was again, that special way he said her name. It made Crystal's nervous system tingle, her fingers and toes curl.

Throat strangely tight, she heard herself whisper, 'Brent, I——'

'Goodnight, Crystal.'

CHAPTER NINE

'AH, COFFEE,' said Roger next morning, welcoming Mrs Carlyle's fragrant-smelling brew. 'Thanks a lot. We need something to prod our brains into action.' The housekeeper smiled as she left them. 'Now come along, you two women, dig even deeper and give me a name. Skin cream—it's your kind of thing.'

Shirley drank, then shook her head. 'Nothing.'

There was a crunch of wheels on gravel. 'Delivery for Mrs Carlyle,' Roger dismissed.

Crystal drank some coffee, shaking her head too. 'Nothing worth recording.'

'Look, Crystal, *anything's* worth writing down at this stage.'

'Well, it sounds silly, but——'

The door opened. A woman entered, dangling car keys. Definitely not a delivery for the housekeeper, Crystal decided, feeling strangely apprehensive. The newcomer, she felt it in her bones, meant trouble with a capital T.

Roger looked at the girls in turn, mouth turned down but eyes alert, no doubt about it, to the visitor's distinct and arresting femininity.

'My name,' the lady announced, moving into the room, 'is Lula Hayle. I'm a friend of Brent Akerman.'

Roger half stood, sank down, and invited her to take a seat. This she declined, preferring, apparently, to look down upon them, still waving her keys.

'Brent has asked me to keep an eye on you.' She pushed at her shining cap of blonde hair, lifted her beads and let them fall, then ran a hand—no doubt for Roger's benefit, Crystal thought acidly—down the curve of her slender hip.

The deep tan on the lady's skin was startling, showing as it did around her throat and shading down to her plunging neckline, over the graceful arms and, Crystal thought, heaven knew where else.

'I know something about marketing,' Lula Hayle was saying. 'I'm out of a job at present, but I used to own a high-class ladies' dress shop.' She looked at them, one by one, then at the sketches and doodles and crossed-out slogans spread over the desk. 'Brent told me to look out for an opening for myself within the company.' So Brent had succumbed to her coaxing demand, had he, to give her a job? And I know how, Crystal thought miserably. 'And I think,' the lady was saying, 'that I might have found it.'

Oh, heavens, no, not with us! Shirley's frown and horrified expression was saying.

'Mr Akerman's never mentioned you to us,' Shirley pointed out. 'I doubt if he would have wished——'

Crystal glanced at her quickly, sure that Shirley had almost said 'wished you on us'.

'Wished us to take on board a fourth member of the team without prior notice,' Crystal finished, more diplomatically than she felt.

There was no doubting the woman's attractions, she thought, her heart somewhere in her sandals. If this slender, curvaceous siren-type really was Brent's lady-friend, as it had seemed from the telephone conversation she had heard that evening in Brent's hotel room, then he could only be playing with the person called Crystal Rose, as indeed he played with her name at every opportunity.

Lula took the seat beside Roger at last, putting her keys away.

'One of the best ways to launch a product,' she offered, 'is to arrange a reception and invite would-be interested parties to attend.' She glanced around and seemed to be pleased with her apparently receptive audience. 'Representatives from department stores, beauty salons, fashion houses, shops that specialise in the sale of products that enhance feminine attractiveness.'

'Fine,' said Roger over-heartily. 'Thanks for the advice.'

'Of course,' Lula added, 'when the time is right I'll make the arrangements. I have many contacts in that field.' She pulled towards her the paper and notepads covered with scrawls and crossings-out. 'Thought of a name yet?'

'Yes,' came promptly from Shirley, who seemed to be resenting the intruder's presence more with each passing minute. Crystal and Roger stared at her, knowing they hadn't. 'Er—Care Cream. Or we might choose,' she pretended to concentrate, 'Sure Care.'

The visitor shook her head. Crystal and Roger exchanged glances, knowing that Shirley was deliberately putting Lula off the scent.

'Silken Smooth,' Roger joined in, giving Crystal a 'your turn' signal.

'Er—yes——' Crystal had to think quickly '—Sweet Creams. A dream of a cream. Something like that.'

Lula rose, eyeing them with disdain.

'I have an appointment,' she informed them from the door, and Crystal heard Roger breathe a heartfelt,

'Thank God!'

They listened to her car driving away, then looked at each other, laughter bursting from them.

'Unfortunately,' Shirley commented, 'I don't think we've seen the last of her.'

'And I've just thought of a name!' exclaimed Crystal. 'A real one this time.' She had their attention, paused for effect, then pronounced, 'Peachflower. How about that?'

A short, considering silence. They exchanged testing glances, then Roger's fist hit the air in a victory salute. 'Peachflower. Great! Got it!' he shouted. 'This deserves a celebration.' He kissed them both on their cheeks. 'Closing time's two hours off. Come along, ladies, to the nearest local.'

'Wait for me,' urged Shirley, dashing for the cloakroom.

'Take Shirley,' Crystal said, sinking down. 'I'll finish off what I was doing before Lula Hayle broke my concentration.'

Roger accepted her decision with a nod.

'I visited the lab, Crystal,' he remarked. 'I told them who I was, and that I was working for Worldview like them. I showed them my pass and told them about my degree course in chemistry. They showed a lot of interest and said feel free, then left me to it.'

'Did it help at all?'

'It did. I got the atmosphere,' he grinned, 'smelt the smells. Watched them working. It was great. Sure you won't join us, Crystal? No? OK.' He looked round. 'Ready, Shirley?' He whistled. 'Sweet and cuddly—I bet you're an armful!'

She smiled, seeming pleased with the compliments. 'Like to test your theory?'

They left, laughing, with their arms around each other.

For a long time after the others had gone Crystal sat at her desk, playing around with the name she had thought of. In itself, she reflected, it had potential, but she grew convinced that it could be improved.

Yawning, she decided that coffee might help to keep her awake. She let herself into the main residence, making for the empty kitchen. The housekeeper, she knew, had gone home some time before.

The house was warm from the day's sunshine. Finishing her coffee, Crystal glanced outside and saw that it was growing dark. She yawned again, telling herself that making the coffee had been a useless gesture, since she was so tired that it would have taken a volcanic eruption to bring her thinking processes back to life.

Creeping into the main living-room—creeping because, although Brent was away, his presence was everywhere—she chose a large armchair and closed her eyes for, she promised herself, just a few moments.

She awoke to the sound of a door banging. The fact that it was now dark completely disorientated her. Hearing footsteps, she began to panic. A break-in! she thought, leaping to her feet. It came to her then that she wasn't in fact at home, which meant that she hadn't left a window open again, inviting trouble.

This was Brent's cottage and...it just couldn't—could it?—be Brent returning?

'Mrs Carlyle?' The shout echoed through the empty rooms. 'Are you still here?' The door burst open and light flooded the room, dazzling her. Brent was indeed there, staring as if he couldn't believe his eyes.

Nor can I believe mine, she thought, staring back, stupefied at being woken so suddenly from so deep a sleep. He was as tall, she found, as magnetic, as heartbreakingly attractive as he had been in her dreams. But more solid...and infinitely more tired.

'A reception committee,' was his first faintly acid comment. 'Now that I didn't expect. But I should have known,' he began to move towards her, 'should have guessed that the radar Crystal Rose seems to possess where Brent Akerman's arrival from far-away places is concerned would pick up his signals and that she'd be here to welcome him on his return.'

'I honestly didn't know you were coming back to-night,' she told him. 'I thought coffee would wake me up, help me to think——'

'*Think*? At this time of night? Why aren't you at home?'

'Work,' she answered simply. 'Could I get you something to eat? Tea or coffee? You—you don't like airline food, you told me once.'

'You remember that, Crystal Rose?' He was close enough now for her to pick up his special aroma, see in close-up his unshaven state and, if she had dared, touch his flaring nostrils.

'How—how could I forget?' she heard herself whisper only seconds before his mouth took hers over and speech became impossible. She wasn't in his arms. They were at his sides, but the kiss was devastating, melding them together as mouth sought mouth, and lips and tongues renewed acquaintance, happy to have found each other again.

When his arms came round her at last hers responded swiftly, and even when the kiss was over they stood like statues in each other's embrace.

'Oh, God, Crystal, I'm so tired.' His mouth found her neck and, with his lips against her skin, his head rested on her shoulder. That first time came back to her, when she had thought he had drunk too much and had taken him to her home to recover. 'Jet lagged to my very soul. Thanks, no, I don't want food. Only sleep. And you.'

There was a pained cry inside her. Not me, not out of desperation for a woman, any woman, not merely as a means of seeking refreshment and renewal...

'You must go to bed, Brent,' she said softly, turning him towards the door and leading him to the stairs. 'Will you go up now?'

Without a word he did as she had asked, taking her with him. His arm was round her so firmly that she could not have escaped if she'd tried.

It all came back...the night she'd helped him, in a similar state of exhaustion, from the hotel to her car, then into her house.

In his room, he slumped on to the bed.

'I'll go now, Brent.'

'Stay, will you?'

'But Brent...'

He glanced at his watch. 'Close on midnight. Not safe. Stay, I said.' He got to his feet. 'I'll take a shower. Just don't——' He swayed a little and she held his arm. 'Just don't run away.' He spoke slowly, and with an equal slowness made for his own *en suite*, closing the door.

It was her chance to leave, to run away. She was torn in two, knowing she should, yet longing to obey his command and stay. It was so long since she had seen him, been this close, heard his voice.

Besides, he was right about the lateness of the hour. A cycle ride through empty streets at midnight held no appeal at all. She could sleep in a chair downstairs, then return home first thing for breakfast and a change of clothes.

She ran down to the kitchen and washed the coffee things. That done, she looked about her and wondered where the housekeeper stored the spare bed-covers. She would need something, she realised, to keep out the chill of the night air while she curled up in an armchair.

As she stood irresolutely on the landing Brent emerged from his room and stood regarding her. The hair on his head was still damp from a shower, the mat of hair on his chest likewise. His shirt hung loosely over briefs that did nothing to hide his masculinity. How, she wondered desperately, could she disguise the attraction he held for her? The tug of his body with which her own was urging her to renew acquaintance was overwhelming.

'If you're wondering which bed to use——' he began.

'An armchair will do,' she interrupted quickly.

'——there's room in mine.'

'Thanks, Brent, but no. I——'

'I've showered,' he went on. 'If you'd like to do likewise you'll find fresh towels in the main bathroom.'

It was a way of escape she hadn't thought of. In his jet lagged state, by the time she emerged he'd be in bed and fast asleep.

She was wrong. Having heard the lock turn to let her out, he was in the corridor before her, barring her way down. She had pulled on her blouse, which hung loose over her briefs. The rest of her clothes she carried with her.

'I told you, Brent,' she said worriedly, 'an armchair will be fine. I'm so tired that I'd be able to sleep anywhere tonight.'

He lifted his arms. 'Not so long ago you slept in these.'

He remembered! 'Yes, but—but the circumstances were quite different. That was——'

'On a sofa. Crystal, I have to tell you that the mating instinct and jet lag as deep as I have it have nothing in common. It cancels out a man's need for anything except sleep. Tell me,' with a smile through which the strain showed, 'how is it for a woman when she's as tired as you are?'

'The same. Brent, there's a chair downstairs that looks inviting. Will you please let me——?'

As she was about to pass him her skirt fell from her hands and she tripped on it. His arm came out, breaking her fall. He allowed her to retrieve her skirt, then twisted her round and against him, sweeping her up and carrying her into his room. Ignoring her verbal protests and her kicking legs, he dropped her on to the bed.

'I thought you said you were tired,' she accused, staring up at him, still clutching her clothes.

'I was. I am. But it's astonishing where the strength comes from when a man wants something that's blatantly being denied him. And you, Miss Rose,' he approached her side of the bed, 'were denying me something I wanted very much indeed—your company in my bed tonight.'

She swung her legs and made to escape, but he crossed to the door and turned the key, tossing it into a drawer.

'Come to bed, Crystal,' he said huskily. 'Tonight I will not violate you.' He spoke the word slowly and with an emphasis that rang true. 'I never make love to a woman against her will. Nor would I trespass on another man's territory.'

'I don't know what, or who you mean. If it's Roger——'

'Leave it,' he countered with an edge, taking the clothes from her arms and dropping them on to a chair. 'Are you reassured?'

'Yes,' she whispered, watching him go round to the other side, discarding his shirt and revealing a torso to which regular attention to exercise had contributed a muscular tone and strength, all of which started the meltdown of her senses. He lifted the bed-covers and got in. Since the door was locked, and she had his promise, she had no alternative but to slide in beside him.

'Crystal...' on his elbow, gazing down into her flushed face, he sounded a little hoarse '...restore my faith in the female of the species.' His fingers brushed away the wisp of hair that had fallen across her face, his knuckles skimming her cheek. 'Your transparent honesty, your high personal standards, your beauty, your clear, candid eyes—do you know what they do to a man?'

He didn't seem to want an answer—which, Crystal thought, was just as well, as at that moment she could

not have said a word. The breadth of his shoulders, the
dark whorls across his chest, with whose softness she
had already become familiar, the male desire that showed
in his eyes despite his tired state—they all combined to
beat down her barriers and make her want to reach up
to him, offering whatever he wanted to take from her.
But she kept her arms rigidly at her sides and closed her
eyes to keep her own desire in, opening them again as
he exclaimed, 'If,' his eyes spat fire in the light from the
table lamp, and his hand settled around her neck, 'if you
ever let me down, ever betray my trust in you...'

'Brent, I won't,' her dry throat croaked. 'I'd never do
that.'

'Break that promise, lady,' his jaw thrust forward and
his fingers tightened a fraction, making her just a little
afraid, 'and I'll——' Shifting his palms to her breasts,
he held them as his mouth drowned her senses in a
clamour of need and a frightening, driving desire. If he
held her much longer it was a sensation she knew she
would find it almost impossible to contain.

Drawing away at last, he settled down, to her sighing
relief turning on to his side away from her.

Daylight was creeping into the room when she sur-
faced again. They were face to face, and Brent's arms
were around her. The weight of his leg across her thighs
was heavy but unbearably exciting. The brush of his
breath on her face, the sensation of his flesh against hers
stung her back to full consciousness, and she realised
that she no longer wore her blouse, although she discovered with something like relief that her briefs were
still in place.

He, too, was bare to the waist, but, as with hers, his
scant covering was doing its job lower down. Her body
sang with the exhilaration of their close proximity, her
mind working overtime as thoughts came and went,
about work, about the way her reflexes were responding

so crazily to the male eroticism of the man who held her so possessively, and about how she loved every single thing about him.

He stirred, and her heartbeats accelerated into the fast lane, her pulses tripping as his mouth picked off kisses from her ears, her neck, her shoulders, lingering on her cheek.

'The perfume you use... what is it?' he muttered, his tongue going to work now, skimming, trailing, making shivering paths all around her ears.

'It's—it's not perfume,' she managed between gasps at his caressing incursions, 'although I suppose it is in a way. It's actually the skin cream, the one we're promoting.' She half turned in his arms. 'I thought of a name, Brent. Shall I try it on you?'

'If you must,' he answered with half his mind, the other half being intricately involved in finding new areas of her body to test for response.

'Peachflower.' No response.

Her brain got working on it again, pushing the activities of his hands and his mouth to one side in her mind. She was aware that the name was not quite right. Something was needed to make it sound, more to *look* different, a name to remember...

Her subconscious came up with the answer just as Brent's fingers started to peel away her briefs. Her hands slapped over his, stopping him.

'Peach*fleur*! The first part of the name in ordinary type, the second part in italics. How's that, Brent?'

He growled against her cleft, his mouth moving to take possession of one pink peak after the other. Her body's needs overrode her mind's discovery, leaving her in a rag doll-like acquiescence in his arms.

'There's a heart where a man's heart usually is, but mine is ice right through.' The words echoed hollowly as his statement, made soon after they had met, came back to her. Her hands gripped his shoulders, pushing him away, but he resisted their pressure easily.

He was no longer suffering from jet lag, that much was clear. Something in Crystal panicked. She shouldn't have let her mind distract her from Brent's activities. Before many more seconds had passed his lovemaking would grow more intimate and far harder to resist, until the point was reached where she would be powerless to stop him.

It took all her strength to overcome the whirlpool pull of his body. Her own body wasn't helping her, and she fought against its feverish response to his coaxing, relentless arousal. With a bruising wrench she was free and kicking clear of the covers. She stood, breathing hard, looking down at the solid, near-naked length of him, his bronzed skin a stark contrast to the pale colour of the bedclothes.

Bronzed and glowing—where else recently had she seen skin like that? On Lula Hayle, who was as deeply tanned as Brent. In this case, two and two added up very definitely to make four.

'Miss Hayle—she went with you on your travels!'

His arms upraised themselves to cushion his head, which turned to allow him to gaze with undisguised lust at her own near-naked state.

'So she did,' came the mocking answer. 'So what?'

His eyes weren't sparing her, roaming over her shape until her flesh seemed to sting. It was the way he looked at her, estimatingly, woven through with indolence, that made her reach out for her garments. Even so, he watched as she donned them hurriedly, one by one.

'Do you behave so inhibitedly with all the men whose beds you've shared?' he drawled.

'Beds I've shared? I——' After the way they had lain entwined in the past few hours, he wouldn't believe the truth—that she hadn't shared even Mick's bed. Which was what their quarrel and eventual split had been about. I'll only ever make love *with love*, she'd told him, and the sound of his disdainful laughter still rang in her ears.

'That's my business,' she riposted, which, she realised, was, in Brent's eyes, as good as admitting that she had slept around. Remembering that the door was locked, she hesitated, looking at him.

He stretched lazily, and the potent masculinity of his body hit her all over again. She had to wrench her eyes away as he gestured towards the drawer into which he had tossed the key.

'Help yourself.'

This she did, turning at the door. 'Thanks,' she threw over her shoulder, 'for the night's accommodation. I'm sorry I wasn't as—as *co-operative* and *obliging* as your lady friend no doubt was while you and she were away, but I'm——' she lied, uncaring of any consequences '—*choosy* about the men I allow to—to *violate* me.'

'Why, you——' His teeth snapped as he swung from the bed, striding towards her. 'You'll pay for that, you little bitch!'

He reached out and dragged her to him, putting his mouth on hers with a slam that made her shake. The kiss he took from her—there was no giving about it—was bruising, punitive and intrusive to the point of plunder.

When he thrust her from him she felt as if she had been mauled by a tiger. With the back of her hand to her throbbing mouth, she gazed at him in disbelief that he could inflict such a hurt, not just to her mouth, but to her dignity and her self-respect. Nor could she take back the tears that sprang and overflowed.

Turning from him, she ran down the stairs, letting herself out and cycling home as if she were being chased by a wild animal.

CHAPTER TEN

SEATED in the main office with Roger and Shirley later that morning, Crystal nearly jumped out of her skin at the crash of a door near by.

'Heavens, Crystal, what's wrong with your nerves?' Shirley asked. 'It's only a door banging.'

To Shirley that might have been all, but Crystal knew what it meant—that the owner who was also their boss had decided to make his presence felt. That his mood was bad was obvious, and they looked at each other apprehensively.

'So what've we done wrong?' Roger asked, frowning.

It's not you—I'm the cause, Crystal could have answered, but stayed silent.

They were into discussing media hype and magazine advertisements when an intercom buzzed across the room on Crystal's desk. It was like an invisible stranger invading their privacy, and it took her a few moments to respond.

'Why the delayed reaction?' came the acid tones.

'Because we're not used to disembodied voices interrupting our discussions,' was her spontaneous, and uncensored, rejoinder. She had felt the tremor in her voice, but her listeners had heard only the tartness.

Roger's and Shirley's gasps coincided with the swift intake of breath of the caller.

'Go easy, pal,' Roger prompted quietly, 'for Pete's sake. And ours.'

'Will the three of you please come to my office across the corridor?' The crash of the receiver was a pale imitation of that of his office door.

'What I said was true,' Crystal said, trying to justify herself.

'You could have made it into a joke at least,' was Roger's worried comment as they followed her out.

Brent's jet lag had returned, Crystal noted, and she had forcibly to restrain her instinct to reach out and comfort him. Her mouth still throbbed from the recent onslaught of his and everywhere else he had touched her in the dawn light. Now her body ached with an alien, shocking need of him.

'Please sit down.' He indicated the three upright chairs placed in a row.

His mood was as bad as they had surmised, although whether that too was caused by jet lag or by her parting shot early that morning, she did not dare to guess.

Was this hard, arrogant man, she wondered, really the same as the one she had first met in a corner of the hotel vestibule at the awards dinner? And, similarly jet lagged, behind the scenes after the meeting at which he had regretfully informed the employees of Ornamental You that their days in work were numbered?

And was this the same man in whose arms she had slept and whose bed she had shared only a few hours ago, whose flesh had pressed against hers, whose hands had——?

Roger nudged her arm and she came to her senses. Brent was looking at her with piercing, dark-ringed eyes, his gaze relenting only a fraction as he transferred it to the others.

'As I was saying,' he stated, 'I've brought you in here to listen to a recorded message I found on my answering machine this morning. I'd like your comments.'

He operated the tape deck that stood on his desk, then picked up a pen, tapping it lightly on a blotter.

The voice, silkily feminine, filled the room.

'Darling,' it said, 'this is Lula, as if you didn't know. I've looked in on the group you appointed to handle the promotion of the new skin cream and honestly, Brent, I'm beginning for the first time ever to question your judgement.'

Roger looked at Crystal, and Shirley looked at Roger.

'All right,' Lula's voice continued, 'so it was a benevolent gesture on your part to rescue them from unemployment and the poverty line, but did you really know what you were doing?'

'Of all the——' Shirley began, but Roger stopped her.

'She's misunderstood the situation,' Roger remarked.

'Didn't anybody tell her,' Shirley demanded indignantly, 'that between us we've got quite a lot of experience in promotion and advertising?'

'In my opinion,' the voice went on, 'and I know you still value it, whatever might have happened between us in the past...'

Roger's frown came Crystal's way. I'd have thought, his expression said, that he'd have scrubbed that private comment.

'They're like college kids who haven't a clue about what they're doing.'

'I object,' Crystal cried, 'with all my heart I object to what she's saying. Didn't anyone tell her,' here Brent switched off the tape, 'that not only do we three in our own ways have previous experience in this line, as Shirley says, but we've also taken the marketing course as prescribed by Worldview prior to starting our jobs?'

With a brief nod of acknowledgement, Brent allowed the tape to run on.

'Altruism's OK in its place, Brent,' Lula asserted, 'but in business—yuk!'

Crystal jerked free of Roger's restraining hand. 'How can you sit there,' she cried, 'and listen to——?'

A cynical flick of the eyebrow quietened her.

'Darling,' the voice went on, 'if you won't dismiss them then I'll just have to push my nose in a little further and try and make good the damage I'm sure they're about to do to Ornamental Cosmetics' new product. I'll think up a name——'

'I've got one,' Crystal broke into the monologue, 'you know that. It's Peach*fleur*.'

'Oh, yes,' Brent's voice grew soft, deceptively so, 'I know that.' Was he remembering the moment she had told him of her find? He had been kissing her—the mere thought made her breasts harden—and she'd been twisting in his arms.

'Hey, what's this, then?' Roger murmured under the cover of the recorded message. The tape was stopped.

'You have a comment to make, Betts?'

'Sorry, sir. Just—just that it sounds great.' But Crystal knew he had been questioning the fact that Brent had known of the new name before he and Shirley had heard it.

Brent ran the tape back a little.

'I'll fix a date for a reception,' Lula's voice declared. 'Then I'll perform my public relations act and contact whoever I think will be interested. Bye, darling. Thanks for finding me a niche to push my—elegant, you used to call it—nose in. Call me any time. I'll be waiting.

'We don't need any outside help,' Crystal protested, swallowing her ire at Brent's woman's audacity and lies, but finding that the piercing jealousy she felt stuck firmly in her throat.

'We're doing all the right things,' she went on, 'on our own. We've learnt about marketing, about forming a panel of housewife testers and sending them small samples, then asking them to complete a questionnaire about how they liked or disliked the product. We know you have to get the name known, fix it firmly in the public's mind——'

'Very commendable, Miss Rose.' Her name came sharply, shocking her. 'So far you've all three done well. I stress, *so far*. I think, however,' his eyes settled on all three in turn, 'you would do well to listen to Miss Hayle. She has wide experience in the field of promotion——'

'But we know all about these things,' Crystal broke in agitatedly. 'We've been working very hard, all of us. Those things Miss Hayle said about us—they're so wrong. They're a dreadful misreading of the situation, and of our characters and abilities.'

'Cool it,' Roger whispered, but Crystal ignored his warning.

'How can you listen to her? But of course, you're prejudiced in her favour. You and—she——'

'Be quiet, Crystal,' Roger said aloud, but Brent's anger was already boiling over.

'You're accusing me, Miss Rose,' he snarled, half rising to his feet, 'of letting my judgement be coloured by my private life?'

His private life? Oh, God, she thought, she *is* still his woman and he really has been playing with me . . . I can't bear it . . .

'I'm s-sorry, I take back every w-word.'

A sob caught her unawares, and to her horror it was followed by another. Her body juddered with them and tears clogged her throat. She covered her eyes, feeling the dampness overflowing down her cheeks.

It was all too much—the hours she'd spent in his arms, loving him more every second, then the quarrel, followed by her own biting, unwise comment, then being told—well, as good as—that Lula was still very much part of his life, and that she, Crystal Rose, was merely

a plaything to use or discard on a whim . . . She choked
and sobbed and fought for breath.

An arm came round her, and it was Roger's shoulder,
Roger's chest her forehead was resting against. She felt
him kiss her hair, heard his soothing words, felt Shirley's
rising agitation at the sight of them. Felt the fury of
Brent's anger raying out towards them.

Crystal eased free and turned to Brent, endeavouring
to hide her blotched and swollen face with the handkerchief which, once again on cue, had arrived from somewhere. 'P-please excuse me, Mr Akerman,' she said
thickly, and turned and ran from the office.

For the next two weeks they worked harder than ever.
There had been neither sight nor sound of Brent, and
Crystal could only conclude that he had gone abroad
again.

'What about this for a slogan?' Shirley asked.
'"Whole Body Beauty, Whole Body Glow"?'

'Or what about "Use Ornamental Peach*fleur* and your
skin will love you"?' was Roger's offering.

'Or,' Crystal suggested, '"Skin Prefers Peach*fleur*"?'

'Short and sweet,' Roger approved. 'Now, let's try
them all together. Run them on, shall we, and use them
as blurb in future ads?'

'I think,' commented Shirley, looking around, 'that
we're doing fine *without outside help*, don't you?'

Roger announced one morning, 'Here's a letter from
she who knows it all.'

'Lula Hayle?'

'Who else, Shirley? She says,' he skimmed through it,
then spoke, 'that she's fixed the date for the promotional reception.' He told them the date. 'It's to be held
at the Gemini Palace Hotel in London—haven't I heard
that name somewhere?'

'It's where Brent—I mean, Mr Akerman lives when he isn't here,' Crystal told them.

'That's right,' said Shirley. 'It means we've got three more weeks to draw up the list of guests and get the invitations out.'

'Right. The letter also says,' Roger went on, 'if we still haven't decided on a name she'll get an ad agency on to it. How do we like that, folks?' He returned the letter to its envelope.

'We don't,' said Shirley.

'But,' Roger held up a cautioning hand. 'I think the boss had something when he told us not to dismiss help from that quarter. Let the lady get on with it, I say, and let *us* get out and about and make our contacts and do the job in our own way. Shall we take a vote?'

Reluctantly, Crystal joined the others in raising her hand.

Three weeks on, they met again, sinking exhausted into their office chairs.

'I've hardly had time to breathe,' Shirley sighed.

'I've been wined and dined up to here,' said Roger, indicating his chin.

'I've worn out a dozen pairs of shoes,' Crystal exaggerated with a smile.

'I take it, then,' Roger said, 'that where the media are concerned we're on our way? Advertising space booked in newspapers and magazines? Not to mention TV channels? That's just great. Who's going to contact our self-appointed lady public-relations rep in London?' Looking at the others' reluctance, he sighed. 'OK, folks, will do. The great event draws ever nearer. Any comments?'

'Only that Ornamental Cosmetics have turned up trumps and produced the special miniature jars of cream to distribute to the guests,' Crystal offered.

'That's great!' exclaimed Roger. 'Partners, we're on our way!'

Crystal was restless, unable to forget the pile of work that sat unattended on her desk. It was Saturday, but she could think of no reason why she shouldn't for once go to the office. By the time she arrived Mrs Carlyle, the housekeeper, would in the owner's absence have been to the house and gone.

Crystal hadn't bothered to dress with her usual care. Instead, she had chosen weekend casuals, a pink top with the word 'Peach*fleur*' snaking in white across it—they'd had great fun in designing the emblem—and matching pink cotton trousers with the emblem scattered over the fabric.

As she worked she became aware that the silence was perversely almost as distracting as the others' chatter usually was on weekdays. Until it was broken by the sound of someone whistling.

> There is a lady sweet and kind,
> Was never face so pleased my mind...

The sound stopped abruptly, and Crystal's heart almost leapt from its rightful place. The door was thrust open, while from behind her a breath was expelled, exasperation mixed in with relief.

Still Crystal didn't turn, just sitting there, muscles locked, as shock and pleasure chased each other round and round her nervous system.

Brent was moving into the room. 'I saw the light from the desk lamp,' he said. 'I thought it was an intruder.'

Crystal sat rigidly, longing for the sight of him after so long, but afraid of giving away to him her total delight at his return.

'A few more seconds, and I've had leapt on you, taking you for a burglar.' A waiting silence, then, 'How would you have liked that, Miss Rose?'

He was home again. And that tone—it was back! She had missed it so much, the way he'd had of using her name as an endearment.

She looked at him at last. He, too, was dressed for weekend living, in a dark short-sleeved cotton knit shirt and white cotton trousers. He leant back, arms folded, against Roger's desk. His eyes, faintly shadowed, taunted; his smile teased. His tan was, if anything, deeper, which meant that yet again he had been visiting warmer climes. At least this time she had the consolation of knowing that Lula Hayle hadn't been with him.

Her smile was a little tremulous as his presence dazzled her eyes, his electricity pushing out a million kilowatts and stinging her all over her body.

'I should hate to be a member of the criminal fraternity with you around, Mr Akerman,' she told him.

'Whatever happened to "Brent"?'

'Brent.'

He was looking at her, studying her features. If only that minute gaze meant that he'd missed her as much as she had missed him!

'Where—where did you go this time?'

'Southern hemisphere. A long, long journey back. So I'm having an easy day.' He looked at her more intently. 'You look pale. Why?'

Joke's on me, Crystal thought with irony. That had been no look of love; only an employer's concern for an employee whose salary he paid.

'Hard work,' she said. 'That goes for all of us.'

'You're not meant to push yourself beyond your limits. Are you still helping Betts?'

'Putting his notes on to the computer? Yes. Is there any reason why I shouldn't?'

'Don't we pay you enough?' The tone was half joking, half edged.

'Of course, very well, thank you. It's not that. It's——'

'No need to spell it out.'

'It's not what you think.' But Brent was plainly unconvinced.

High-pitched childish laughter drifted in. Children on the swing? So that was why he had kept it. It could only mean one thing: Lula Hayle must have been married, had a family and then got divorced. It was Saturday, so she'd brought the children over to see the man she was one day going to marry!

'My young nephew and niece,' he said. 'My sister's brought them for the day.'

The relief almost made Crystal feel faint.

She shuffled some papers together and got up. 'I'm sorry, I'm intruding on the family gathering. If I'd known——'

'Will you share our picnic lunch? We thought we'd go down to the river. Or have you got a date?'

Share a picnic lunch with Brent and his family? Crystal's eyes shone. 'No lunch date, but——'

'You've got one for this evening?' His expression gave nothing away.

'Not exactly what you'd call a date. Roger's just bringing me some more work.'

'I get the picture.' Now his expression spoke volumes. 'And staying overnight', she could almost hear him thinking.

'There's no picture to get, Brent.'

'No? I remember not so long ago when you seemed only too glad to cry your eyes out in his arms.'

If only it had been yours! Wasn't it lucky, she thought, that he couldn't read her mind? 'A sort of brotherly comfort, that's all it was.'

'Yeah? I saw his face.'

'Brent? *Brent*!' There were footsteps, and a small boy, three-plus, Crystal estimated, half helped, half pushed his tiny sister, who was coping determinedly with the swaying whims of a baby-walker, into the room. 'Look at Kathy! She's——'

The boy saw Crystal and halted in the doorway. The little girl came on, tripping on a length of woven matting and sprawling sideways. Her cries were more of annoyance than pain as Brent extricated and held her, tolerating her tiny fingers as they clutched at his hair.

'I'm Ray,' the boy said brightly. 'What's your name?'

'Crystal,' she answered with a smile.

'Rose,' supplied his uncle.

'*Two* names? Aren't you lucky!' Ray tried them out. 'Crystal Rose. Crystal Rose.'

Crystal smiled broadly at his uncle. 'He's got the family trait, playing with my name.'

The uncle's eyes narrowed, roving over her speculatively. 'I'd like to play with the owner of that—— Ow!' as his niece, on cue, pulled a tuft of his hair, and Crystal laughed.

'Brent?' came through the half-opened connecting door. 'Where's that brother of mine? Oh, sorry. Hi,' as a pair of grey eyes, plainly another family characteristic, alighted on Crystal. 'You might be...?' She looked at Brent, nudging him.

'Mina, this is Crystal.'

'Crystal Rose, Crystal Rose,' intoned the small boy.

'Crystal—my sister, Wilhelmina. Wilhel for short.'

'*Mina*,' came the exasperated correction. 'He used to torment me with that as a child. Um—you'll be—er——' she sought for brotherly guidance '—your—er—friend, Brent?'

'Employee,' Crystal pointed out, feeling the need to explain. 'I really came this morning to catch up on my work, but——'

'She's coming with us,' said Brent, bending to fix his niece back into the baby-walker. 'She's overdone the overtime, and she needs some good fresh air to bring her colour back.'

Crystal's heart leapt at the thought of the afternoon ahead.

'Good.' The slightly younger grey eyes appeared to approve of her brother's 'er—friend'. 'What a good—um—employer you are, Brent,' Mina added with sisterly sarcasm and, plainly, disbelief at Crystal's explanation of her role in Brent's life.

Mina led the way into the main residence, while the children trailed after the grown-ups.

'You must let me help,' Crystal declared.

'Come and talk to me while I make the sandwiches,' Mina invited. 'You can see to the tea and coffee flasks if you like. Brent—OK?' Sister seemed to need brother's agreement to taking his 'employee' into the bosom of the family.

Brent nodded without looking up, seemingly absorbed in the task of helping his niece master the art of taking one adventurous step after the other.

Mina spread the bread and inserted the fillings, while Crystal busied herself with filling the vacuum flasks.

'Tell me something I'm dying to know,' Mina said. 'You know, purely for family reasons, although I do admit it's no business of mine. But are you really just——?'

'Brent's employee?' Crystal interposed, laughing. 'I—well, I—we——'

'OK,' Mina laughed with her. 'I get it.' She wrapped the sandwiches and searched for the biscuit box.

'Would you tell *me* something?' Crystal asked. 'Don't if it's intruding on private matters.'

'I'll take a guess. Lula? Yes? Well, whatever there was has been over for a long time now.' Mina took the filled flasks from Crystal, who watched as the bags were expertly packed. 'Brent and she were definitely considering marriage. Well, to the extent that she wore his ring.'

Mina paused to push a handful of paper tissues into a zip pocket of one of the bags.

'Then,' she continued, 'he discovered she was having a parallel affair with someone else. When Brent confronted her with it she admitted that she was and, to make matters worse, that she'd intended carrying it on even after they were married. She wouldn't mind, she actually said—can you believe it?—if he did the same. It was the modern way, wasn't it? she said.'

'And Brent?'

'Told her what she could do with her modern ideas. To him marriage meant monogamy, he said—or so he told me—not a kind of closet bigamy. She went off in a huff.' Mina chuckled. 'She kept the ring. It was an expensive one, and Brent's told me he's seen her flaunting it even now. He—er——' She looked askance at Crystal, seeming to wonder if she should continue. 'He did say at the time—he was *very* angry, furious in fact—that he'd never propose marriage to any other woman, not even if she was Venus come to life. I hope I'm not putting my big foot in it, if you get me.'

'Of course not.' Crystal spoke so emphatically that Mina looked at her. 'I wouldn't look for permanence in a man like Brent,' she declared untruthfully. 'He's too...' too much like a dream beyond my reach, she almost said '...he's so...' handsome and fine and everything a girl like me could want but never have, she longed to say, but didn't. 'Anyway, I've——' She cleared her strangely hoarse throat, then forced out the bitter lie, 'I've got someone else. A—a colleague.'

Mina looked half relieved, half disappointed and curiously half unbelieving. A sigh came softly from her as she tested the bags for weight. 'Pity. He could do with a good woman in his life.' Raising her voice, she yelled, 'Baggage handler wanted this second!'

Brent appeared just a little too fast for Crystal's peace of mind. Had he heard their conversation? Most of all, her blatant lie regarding Roger's place in her life?

His expression was so bland, so relaxed that Crystal took comfort from it. The children trailed after him as he scooped up the bags and carried them outside.

The afternoon passed on wings. Crystal felt so happy that she decided she had something in common with Icarus who, as mythology had it, had flown too close to the sun. She hoped, though, that *her* 'wings' wouldn't melt. She would hate the terrible fall back to earth, let alone the crash landing when she reached it.

The weather was kind, the sun bringing out the mischief in Ray as he alternately crawled over his surprisingly good-tempered uncle and played too roughly with his little sister.

Mina dealt capably with her small son's antics, repacking the bags and putting the uneaten sandwiches into a paper bag.

'Come on, young man,' to her son as she lowered her daughter into the push-chair, 'let's go for a walk along the river and feed the ducks.'

'What about Brent and—and Crystal Rose?' the boy asked, hanging back.

Mina's being diplomatic, Crystal thought, wishing she wouldn't.

'He and Crystal will be here when we come back,' his mother stated, allowing no argument.

Or, Crystal wondered, had brother whispered in sister's ear, dropping a hint?

Whatever, she would never know, and pulled her bag towards her, combing her hair, hoping Brent didn't have other ideas, because if he so much as touched her...

All afternoon he had allowed himself to be distracted by his sister's children, showing no special interest in her, Crystal. Except, she had to admit, for the occasional sideways glance, letting his eyes wander over her trousered legs and dwelling on the shape her well-fitting top had done nothing to hide.

She had turned her gaze fully on to him, hoping to convey her annoyance at his audacity, but he'd merely smiled broadly and continued playing with the children. Occasionally he had yawned as though his body clock was telling him the wrong time of day.

Now he lay full length beside her, pulling at the meadow grass and throwing it down. He turned his head and a few taut moments passed. Then, as if he couldn't stand it a moment longer, he jackknifed up and seized her comb, dropping it and pulling her down beside him.

'A man,' he said through gritted teeth, 'jet lagged or not, can stand so much, and no more. Flaunting your golden hair, your beauty——'

'No, I wasn't,' Crystal protested, struggling.

'—sitting there all afternoon,' Brent placed himself on top of her and gathered her wrists, forcing them above her head, 'like a flaming ice maiden!'

'That's—that's a contradiction in terms,' she corrected, laughing up at him.

'You think you're clever, don't you?' he responded, nipping her nose with his white teeth, then, heeding her protests, kissing it better.

'Don't do that,' she cautioned. 'The others might come back.'

'Not yet. I told my sister, give us fifteen minutes alone. We synchronised our watches.'

Crystal gasped at his deliberate setting up of the situation. 'You think of everything, don't you?'

'I do my best, my little peachflower,' he riposted, grinning.

'You've just used——'

'The name of the new product. So what?' He half rolled off her, tracing the word 'Peach*fleur*' printed boldly across her cotton top. In doing so, his finger pressed against her breasts and, narrow-eyed, he watched them harden under his touch.

He ran a finger down her scarlet cheeks. 'It suits you, Miss Rose.' Her name had become an endearment again. 'Your skin's so smooth that you're one lady who doesn't need its services.' He gazed down at her and, her hands still imprisoned, she could only gaze back, loving his smile with its faintly cynical curve, his forceful jaw, the way his dark hair had been ruffled by his nephew.

No man, she thought, should possess eyelashes that long, or a mouth so sensual that a woman longed with all her being to place her own upon it.

'Go on,' he taunted, 'kiss me. I can see you're longing to. *Kiss me*,' he leaned over her, 'or I'll——'

Lifting her head, she was just able to reach his mouth, placing a thistledown kiss upon it.

He growled his frustration and took her mouth with his, grinding into it, then gentling it into a caress, playing with her lips until they parted. The kiss became demanding, invasive and...intoxicating, swamping her senses and drawing from her a passionate response.

At last he released her hands and they swung, delighted with their freedom, to wrap around his shoulders, his neck, her fingers burrowing in his hair, while her body grew limp with longing for his total domination.

'The ice maiden melts,' he said huskily, eyelids drooping. 'Do you know, I wonder, how beautiful you are? And, madam,' huskily, 'are you aware of how near we are to——?'

'Brent, they're coming back!' she exclaimed. 'Can't you hear them?'

Swearing faintly, he rolled away, pulling her with him into a sitting position. By the time Mina dropped beside them, all that was left of their togetherness was their finger-to-finger contact.

This Mina must have noted, since she commented, with an expression as mischievous as that of her small son, 'The fresh air must have done your *employee* good this afternoon, Brent. It's certainly brought the colour to her cheeks.'

Too late, Crystal tried to hide her hectic flush with the backs of her hands. Brent contented himself with pushing a playful fist in his sister's direction, then smiled inscrutably at the distant scene.

Brent took Crystal home, along with her bicycle. He wheeled it into the hall and made for the living-room as if he had lived there for years.

'Tea, Brent?' she asked as he wandered round, his overpowering presence making the room seem smaller than it really was. 'Coffee?'

'Thanks, but neither.' He smiled over his shoulder as he wandered to her desk, flicking through a pile of Roger's notes. He yawned, his body appearing to be arguing with a mind that would not let him do the sensible thing and sleep.

'Shouldn't you,' he broke into the silence, 'be more discreet with his work?'

Crystal frowned. 'When I've printed out his notes, keep them under lock and key, you mean? They're just notes of lectures, aren't they? If he'd ever asked me to, of course, I would.' A long pause while his attention seemed caught by a passage in the notes and a curious foreboding formed inside her. 'I—I don't understand a word, Brent, of what I'm putting on to the screen.' Why should she suddenly feel on the defensive? She had nothing to hide. A faint shiver coursed through her. The atmosphere seemed, strangely, to have gone cold. 'You?'

'Understand them? Not my subject. Ever heard,' he turned, looking at her intently, 'of Halmanner Beauty Products?'

'Just a guess—another cosmetics company?'

'Right. Ornamental Cosmetics' new rivals. They're out to beat Ornamental by any method, by fair means or foul.'

'Oh.' How else, Crystal asked herself, should she react to such an oddly gratuitous piece of information?

He glanced outside. 'You're expecting Betts. Or so you said.' He turned and yawned again, covering his mouth.

'You look tired, Brent,' Crystal ventured. 'I suppose it's not surprising, after all those hours you spent in the air.'

'Tired, am I? Not too tired for...' He held her shoulders and searched her face. 'Yes, even for... A man's only human.'

He sank on to the sofa, pulling her with him and into the semicircle of his arm. 'You wouldn't believe, Crystal Rose, what I've missed. This,' his fingers turned her chin and his mouth placed tiny, tantalising kisses over her lips, then inhaled deeply at the base of her throat, 'your own special scent, and this,' his hand made a path for itself beneath her cotton shirt, finding with a sureness that went with a growing familiarity of the terrain the swelling, hardening mounds beneath, 'the touch of your breasts,' they moved down to her waist, 'the feel of your skin...'

By now she was helpless in his arms, returning his kisses, her arms around his neck clinging for dear life.

'And wanting more, all that we shared this afternoon, but much, much more,' he added thickly, his hand burrowing below her loosened waistband to stroke the throbbing softness of her stomach. 'If I asked, Crystal Rose, would you give?'

Remember, she warned herself, this man has no heart—yes, he has, but it's made of ice. Didn't he tell you so himself? But she no longer had any control over her reflexes, ignoring as they were the rein she tried to put on them. Nor could she answer his question, since his mouth had claimed hers again, harder this time, his kiss more insistent, more probing, more demanding.

'But,' he lifted his lips from hers, to her dismay reaching up and disentangling her arms, putting her away from him, 'your lover is coming.' He disregarded her unspoken denial and got to his feet. 'And some while ago I made you a promise that I wouldn't encroach on his private property.'

'But——' Despairing, she looked the whole length of him. What was the use of denying his assertion? He wouldn't believe her, would he, if she did?

He looked down at her, hands in his pockets, expression unreadable. 'Thanks, Miss Rose, for your company today. And thank you,' too softly, too smoothly for her peace of mind, 'for allowing me to indulge my male needs even if only to a small degree, after my enforced abstinence from the pleasures that only the female of the species can give a man like me.'

It was like a slap in the face. He had meant his words to hurt, and hurt they did. The pain they inflicted was so great that she launched herself at him, fists at his chest, his arms, wherever they could reach. He fended them off with consummate ease.

'Roger is *not* my lover,' she cried as he turned to go. 'Just a friend. Don't you understand?'

Now he was in his car, fastening his seat-belt...leaving, just like that, after all the laughter and the kisses they'd shared that afternoon? Leaving, without even saying goodbye?

CHAPTER ELEVEN

CRYSTAL took a few moments off to catch her breath, looking around with no small measure of satisfaction. Taking a couple of sips from the glass of wine she had been carrying around with her for most of the evening, she told herself, for heaven's sake, relax!

The reception was going with a swing, wasn't it? But why hadn't Brent come? Hadn't he considered it a worthy enough event to put himself out to attend? One, after all, that crowned the tremendous effort they had put in over the weeks and months they'd been working on the project. Even so, her eyes started to search again. All week she had longed for a word, a phone call, but there had been nothing.

Roger joined her, Shirley in tow. 'We've made it, partners,' he said between mouthfuls, gazing delightedly at the chattering, laughing throng. 'You have to admit that Lula's done a great job.'

'Not only Lula. What about us?' Shirley corrected. 'Do you know,' she helped herself from Roger's plate, piled high, 'I've met more big names and celebrities this evening than I've done in the whole of my life before? Have a bite, Crystal,' she added, indicating Roger's plate.

'Thanks, but I won't.' Crystal took another sip from the glass of wine. She didn't feel hungry. Brent still hadn't come and, despite her firm decision not to let this fact upset her, her appetite was non-existent.

'One of the guests, Roger,' Shirley pointed discreetly, 'the tall grey-haired man over there——'

'Distinguished-looking, I think they call it,' Crystal broke in, sipping from her glass.

'Crystal and I have been talking to him for ages. He seemed terribly interested in how we'd gone about the project, didn't he, Crystal?'

'He said lots of nice things. In fact, he complimented us on how we'd gone about marketing Peach*fleur*.'

Roger nodded. 'I know the chap you mean. I had a talk with him, too. Went out of his way to attract my attention. Said his name was Hal Mannering. I couldn't place him, but I didn't like to say so. He seemed very interested in the fact that I'm studying for a degree, and that chemistry was my subject. I said it had helped me—us—cope with the project.'

'I bet you didn't tell him,' Crystal smiled up at Roger, 'that I'm helping you get that degree by——'

'Bringing order out of the chaos of my notes,' Roger broke in with a grin. 'As a matter of fact, I did. One of my girlfriends, I said.' He smiled at Shirley's troubled face. 'Although you and I, Crystal, know you're not,' he added.

Shirley's smile held both relief and pleasure.

'He asked if I had a business card, so I gave him mine, and yours and Shirley's. We agreed, didn't we, to carry each other's around and distribute them if and when the occasion arose?' He glanced at his watch. 'Ten more minutes to the promotional video. Be prepared, ladies, to see yourselves on the big screen. I've had a preview, and you look just great. Your complexion looks A1,' he made a circle with his forefinger and thumb, 'and,' he smiled at them each in turn, 'you both look beautiful.'

'Thanks to Peach*fleur*,' they intoned together, then dissolved into laughter.

'Mr Betts?' Roger turned, eager for fresh contacts. 'Ah,' said the newcomer, hand extended. 'Happy to meet you. My name's Jimmy Miston.' He invited Roger to take a step or two to one side.

Crystal and Shirley exchanged glances, Shirley shrugging and proceeding to empty Roger's plate, putting it aside. Roger turned back to them a few minutes later, the man called Miston having disappeared into the crowd.

'What was that all about?' Shirley asked, head on one side.

'Dunno.' Roger looked genuinely puzzled. 'Know something? He as good as offered me a job. What did I have in mind to do when all this razzmatazz was over? I said I hadn't given it a thought, what with my studies, plus all the work we've had to put in to launch this product successfully.'

'Then?' asked Crystal, as puzzled as Roger was.

'He said he worked for a company—small, as yet— Halmanner Beauty Products. Owned by none other than our tall, distinguished guest, Mr Hal Mannering. This guy,' Roger took a business card from his pocket, 'Jim Miston, said his company had it in mind to create a new skin cream, then promote it the way we've done.'

'By fair means or foul,' Brent had said. Was this what he had meant, had been trying to warn her about?

'He didn't mean as a rival to Peach*fleur*?' Crystal asked worriedly.

'I'd say it sounded like it,' Shirley responded, her tone echoing the anxiety in Crystal's.

'Whatever,' Roger shrugged. 'He also said that, in view of my,' he corrected himself hastily, '*our* success with this little lot, his firm would like to be the first to offer me a similar job. Name my own salary, he said.'

The girls stared at him as he, in turn, stared unseeingly at the laughing, chattering groups.

'You look a bit shell-shocked, Roger,' Crystal commented with a strained smile. In some way she could not understand, their success and that of the promotional party had been just a little diminished. It also worried her that Roger seemed troubled, as if he had not told them everything. 'Would you consider an offer like that?'

'Dunno,' he answered, still bemused. 'Got to put my studies first now. When I graduate—well, who knows? Ah, well,' he brightened at last, 'there's this little lot to bring to a conclusion before any of us starts to think actively about our future. Agreed?'

'Agreed,' they echoed, at Roger's suggestion shaking on it.

The guests continued to swallow the fine wines and consume with relish the lavish spread the parent company had provided, turning with interest to face the shallow platform as the lights dimmed and romantic music, thoughtfully chosen by the three of them, filled the large room.

The film lasted three minutes, having been timed to the second by Roger, who had directed it, with the assistance, at Ornamental Cosmetics' expense, of a professional producer.

Lula stepped forward from the crowd and mounted the platform. The assembled company fell silent.

'This whole project,' she told them, in Crystal's view quite unnecessarily, 'was conceived in its entirety,' her voice as seductive as her wrap-around satin-bright gold-coloured dress, 'as a "job creation" activity by Brent Akerman, the philanthropic and, yes, compassionate chief executive of Worldview. You see, these young people,' her hand waved gracefully towards the three concerned, 'had all lost their jobs. We at Worldview——'

'Since when,' Roger commented through the corner of his mouth, 'has that lady been elevated to the company's hierarchy?'

'—are delighted with their achievements,' Lula went on, 'and, I'm sure, so are you.'

The applause was punctuated by cheers as the guests' eyes turned towards Crystal and her companions.

'She's squashing us flat,' Crystal whispered angrily.

'Putting us down,' agreed Shirley. 'And I know why—she's jealous!'

There was generous applause and cries for the group to take a bow. They filed on to the platform, Shirley leading, followed by Crystal and Roger. Linking hands, they bowed.

'They've done wonders,' came a voice from the audience. 'I'd give 'em a job any day.'

Searching the upturned faces, Crystal saw that the speaker had been Hal Mannering, the man to whom they had spoken earlier and who had seemed so interested in them. She felt like hugging him for his boost to their ego, and for contradicting so effectively Lula Hayle's patronising introduction of them a few moments ago.

Amid renewed applause, flowers were carried on to the platform—a bouquet for Shirley, a large buttonhole for Roger, while Crystal became aware of a box being placed in her hands.

'Open it!' came from the audience, so open it she did, stooping to lift from the tissue an arrangement of red roses rising from out of—it couldn't be, she thought dazedly, could it?—a crystal rose bowl!

Tears dimmed her eyes. It was a replacement for the rose bowl that had been smashed beyond repair when the shop had been ransacked. Only one person in the whole world could have done this, she realised, and he wasn't there. Was he? Mistily her eyes searched the room. *He was.*

He stood at the back, arms folded, leaning against the wall. She wanted to jump from the platform and run to him.

'Speech,' the guests were demanding, 'speech!'

'Crystal?' It was Roger whispering.

'You do it, please,' she begged, too overcome to oblige. Carefully she replaced the precious bowl in its box, cradling it in her arms.

Roger rose to the occasion, drawing forth yet more applause, then leading the way down. Crystal was only dimly aware that Lula had remounted the platform and was accepting with exaggerated astonishment her own bouquet of flowers.

It signalled the end of the party, and the noise level rose accordingly. In her eagerness to reach the man for whom she had searched the whole evening, Crystal hugged the precious box to her and fought her way round one reformed group after another to reach her goal.

Someone had tapped Brent on the shoulder, apparently passing on a message. He nodded and turned to go. Crystal stifled a cry and pushed even more forcefully through circles of people who, in a mere few seconds, had put themselves in her path.

Reaching the corridor, she saw him walking at speed toward the lift.

'Bre-nt...' His name was torn from her, echoing from high ceiling to tiled floor.

Some distance away though he was, he must have heard, since he turned, seeing her. A moment's hesitation, then his hand came out. She flew to his side, clutching the box, transferring it to her arm and putting her hand in his.

If her pleasure showed through, if her happiness at seeing him again was floodlighting her eyes, she didn't care. She was with him again... and he had given her this wonderful gift.

'I wanted to thank you——'

He put a finger to his lips. The lift was there, half filled, and he led her into it. In silence they ascended, with frequent stops, to his floor, where he pulled her after him. The lift whirred on its way.

'My room's lower down,' she managed before he operated a lock and invited her in. 'We passed it. Shirley and Roger and I booked in for the night, knowing we'd be late.'

It was, of course, Brent's suite they were in and which, the last time she had been there, had been his only home. A glance into the bedroom brought back memories that deepened the already high colour in her cheeks.

'Please excuse me,' he said, lifting the phone and taking the call, which, judging by the light that flashed on the instrument, had been waiting for him.

As he talked, Crystal put down the box and wandered round, admiring all over again the tasteful furnishings, the bathroom suite with its flattering lighting and, most of all, the view over London.

The call ended and she swung round, a smile lighting her eyes. 'Brent, the rose bowl. How can I thank you?'

He opened his arms. 'The well-tried method would do, Miss Rose.'

The seductive softness in his musical voice was her undoing, and, abandoning all restraint, she rushed into his embrace. Her arms wrapped themselves around his middle and her ear pressed against the breadth of his chest, picking up the rhythmic hammering that raised hopes in her that his heart might not be, after all, just a solid block of ice.

He rocked her one way, then the other, and she went with him, laughing against his rib-cage.

Her head went back, her bright eyes finding his. 'When did you arrive, Brent?'

'About halfway through. I saw the film. I noticed the assembled company's gratifying interest in that film, not to mention the way they continued gorging themselves all through it at Worldview's expense.'

Crystal frowned up at him. 'That's what it was all about, surely?' She started to pull away, but he held her firmly. 'I mean, we were told that where the reception was concerned money was no object. And the little pots of Peach*fleur* we distributed—they were approved, too, by the powers that be. Which I assumed to mean Mr

Brent Akerman, since all along he's been our mentor and backer.'

She stole a glance upward and discovered a smile hovering, and something else in his eyes that made her nervous system go into a breath-robbing spin.

'So quick she is to take umbrage and get on her soapbox!' His eyes were hooded, his hands pushing under the pink and white Peach*fleur* top, finding what they were seeking and moulding them, bringing twin flares to her cheeks. 'This is where I want her, in my arms in the privacy of my room, not proclaiming her grievances to the world.'

'Brent, I——' Tell him no, part of her was insisting, otherwise not only will you burn your fingers, but also the whole of your body and your life will go up in flames. Heeding that inner warning, she tried again. 'Brent, this isn't—we can't—I don't——'

His lips were nuzzling her ear, her throat, his hands pushing into her hair. 'I, Crystal Rose,' he muttered against her mouth, 'will take the necessary preventive steps.'

That was fine, she thought, and it was totally understandable that he should want to avoid any possible and shattering consequences. But he still didn't understand, did he? And she began to despair of getting through to him that there had to be a first time for everything and that this . . .

He was undermining her power to resist, and, since she didn't want to resist anyway, his kisses easily demolished the few barriers that had managed to withstand his onslaught. She found herself lifting her arms, pressing her body against the angles of his, accepting his kisses as if she couldn't live another moment without them.

He gazed down at her radiant face, and his lips uttered an order she couldn't have disobeyed even if she'd wanted to. 'Kiss me.'

She had to stand on tiptoe, and even then she only reached his chin. He relented sufficiently to ease her task by lowering his head and waiting for her mouth to do his bidding.

At last it found its target, and as her lips fluttered against the hard line of his his mouth took over, tongue flicking her lips into parting, allowing him entry to her inner sweetness and taking into himself her gasps at the audacity of his invading tongue.

With quick, sure movements he divested himself of his jacket and tie, unbuttoning his shirt, then he swung her into his arms, thrusting into the bedroom. Sliding her through his hands beside the bed, he tugged the cotton top over her head, making short work of disposing of the lacy covering beneath. Then she stood, naked to the waist, her heated, pulsing flesh entirely at the mercy of his erotic gaze.

'Has anyone, my little peachflower,' he said huskily, bending down, his breath warm on her burgeoning shape, his mouth and tongue robbing her of the power to breathe, 'told you how beautiful you are the way nature formed you?'

'Brent,' she whispered, hardly able to speak, 'I—I——'

His head came up, his eyes glittering with—what, desire? Anger? If so, what had she done wrong?

He swung her round so that her back was against him, her over-sensitive skin rubbing against the finely curling mat that sprawled across his chest. When his hands came up to cup her breasts, playing with their rosy peaks until the ache in her loins became almost unbearable, he said into the hollows of her neck, 'You ran after me. You called out to me. When I stretched out my hand to you, you came. Why, Crystal?'

'To—thank you, Brent,' she answered hoarsely, 'for the crystal rose bowl.'

His teeth nipped her shoulder, making her yelp. 'Now tell me the truth.'

She shook her head and rubbed her hair against his chest, arching against him in her agony and ecstasy at his persistent arousal, involuntarily thrusting her flesh more firmly into his tantalising grasp.

Whispering, she confessed, 'I'd been looking out for you all evening.'

He spun her round, locking his hands around her throat. 'You missed me?'

She nodded, loving the shape of his head, the determination in his chin and mouthline, his eyebrows, which brooded over his unfathomable gaze.

'Maybe I did,' she deliberately prevaricated.

'Your emotional bank account—it's still empty? Does it still have cash-flow problems?'

How could she answer him—with a lie, which would go against her principles? Or the truth, that he had, as no other man had ever done, filled that 'account' to overflowing? Which statement would, in view of his determination never again to make a commitment to a woman, be tantamount to saying goodbye to him?

'If so,' his eyes seemed strangely hard, 'maybe I could pay something into it?' She gazed up at him steadily, taking refuge in silence. 'I warn you, Crystal Rose, it might be in foreign coinage——'

'What—what use would that be to me?' she choked, understanding his meaning, that no amount of lovemaking would make her any more to him than a passing fancy.

'Roger Betts...' came harshly from him, in his altered mood his fingertips pressing painfully into her flesh. 'Where does he stand in your life?'

'Brent, he doesn't figure in it at all.' She gritted her teeth against his relentless, burning arousal. 'You just have to believe me.'

But did he? He gave no clue. Had he still not forgiven womankind after Lula's two-timing of him in the past?

Hands on her waist, he shook her. 'Look at me.' She obeyed.

She did not know what he saw in her eyes, but his own softened, and in a few swift movements he divested her of the rest of her clothing, squatting on his haunches to free her feet from her Peach*fleur* trousers and taking the chance to implant a series of kisses that made her gasp in their intimacy and their profound effect.

Then, ridding himself of his own covering, he scooped her up and dropped her on to his bed. His mouth came down, blotting out all reality and filling her mind with dream music and misty shapes, drawing from her body such responses as she had never realised she had.

All those years they had lain dormant, waiting for the right man, and she was glad, glad to have waited for this—this sensation of feeling, of sharing and giving, and loving this man whom she loved beyond words, beyond belief.

'Brent, Brent, I——' she pleaded, her head moving wildly from side to side. Her voice sounded strange, not really seeming to belong to her as her lips roamed his chest, his neck, his arms, those strong, muscled arms that held her and manoeuvred her, his hands as they brought from her cries of pleasure and purest happiness.

Now she was almost his, feeling him coming into her, hearing him ask, 'Crystal?' His actions were slowed, his entry made with a care that brought tears of gratitude to her eyes, then, as though he could restrain himself no longer, he was possessing her with a thrust and rhythm that caught her breath in her lungs as time stood still and she soared with him to the final fulfilment.

'Crystal...' he had slept with his head on her breasts, and awoken to caress them with his lips '...if I hurt you——'

'No, no, Brent,' she kissed his forehead, 'you were wonderful.'

'Don't you mean,' he lifted himself on to an elbow, smiling down at her, 'that *it* was wonderful?'

Was that what he wanted her to say, proving to him that it was the experience that had brought her such joy and not the fact that it was he who had made such incredible love to her?

The frown must have pleated her forehead, since he made to smooth it away. 'What are you telling me?' he asked softly.

Something he must never know. What would be the use? If they had an affair it would end. Hadn't he told his sister that he would never propose marriage again? And wasn't it permanency that she, Crystal, would want with this man she loved so deeply, because parting from him would leave her future, her whole life in ruins?

He began to kiss her all over again and her body succumbed of its own accord, alive as it was from its recent experience in his arms, and wanting more of his loving, and more...

She awoke to the beginnings of daylight and the impact of stark reality. Here and now she must make the decision that would affect the rest of her life.

Looking at Brent's face in repose, the character and the strength it held even in sleep, the power implicit in his bare shoulders, the chest against which her head had rested after... Her heart, she was sure, was tearing free of her body and leaving her lifeless, her future bleak and empty. But this she had to do.

As he slept on beside her she slid from under his thigh flung across her, lifting herself in tiny movements from the arm that lay beneath her, imprisoning a breast, and rolled from the bed, gathering her clothes and pulling them on. Holding under her arm the box containing the precious rose bowl, she tiptoed to the door and slipped silently out, hearing the lock click behind her.

She gave thanks that the lift came quickly and was empty. Her own room seemed miles away, but no one came along as she let herself in, although from far away there were sounds of the hotel coming to life. Her bed, untouched, seemed to reproach her, but she stifled the urge to untidy the bed-covers and make it seem as if she had occupied it.

Opening the box, she extracted the rose bowl and saw how much in need of water the red roses were. This she rectified by means of a glass from the bathroom, and placed the bowl and its sweet-smelling contents on a coffee-table near the window.

The shower soothed her still vibrant body, the water's lukewarm temperature freshening her skin and causing a faint shiver to course through her. It wasn't only the coolness that wrapped around her as she stepped out that caused it. It was the faint apprehension that had descended upon her as she had closed Brent's door and gone away from him that troubled her unduly.

She loved him more than ever, there was no doubt about that, but her fingers stung from the fire she had knowingly pushed them into. *There could be no future for their new relationship.* Be honest and admit, she reprimanded her protesting self as she dressed, that from the start you knew that. Too alert now to consider sleeping the couple of hours that were left until breakfast, she dressed, repacking her belongings.

Outside the traffic had never stopped. It was lighter in density, perhaps, but increasing by the minute. The sun was high in the sky, which was where her spirits and her heart had been all through those hours she had spent in Brent's arms. Now they were down there under the wheels of those relentless vehicles.

When the gentle tap came she ran to the door. All her good resolutions to break free now before it was too late were thrown to the winds. Brent had come!

It was Roger. Her spirits nosedived as she forced a welcoming smile.

'Crystal, where've you been?' he asked. 'Shirley and I tried to contact you until gone midnight. If I hadn't seen you make a mad dash from the party and followed you into the corridor I'd have thought you'd gone missing.' He saw the neat state of the bed. 'They haven't been in to make it already? You should complain to the——'

As the possible explanation dawned Roger exclaimed, 'You haven't slept in it, have you? Crystal,' he frowned worriedly, 'you've been with...him? There's no future in it, you realise? He's playing with you, pal, he has to be. A man like that, he's probably got a computer print-out as long as your arm of assorted females' addresses. OK, OK,' he soothed as she made to protest, even though she secretly acknowledged that he was probably right, 'I didn't come here to quiz you on your private life. Anyway, I've suspected for a long time that there was something going on between you and that guy.'

She felt it was only fair to tell him. 'Not really until now, Roger.'

He walked to the window, walked back, in that time arranging a smile that cancelled out the disappointment he was plainly feeling.

'I never honestly thought,' he said, 'that I had a snowball in a furnace's chance with you. No, what I came about was something I kept to myself yesterday evening.'

He prodded at the carpet with his foot. He doesn't really want to tell, Crystal guessed.

At last he went on, 'That guy, Jimmy Miston—remember?—he said other things. Since we three are partners—I've already told Shirley—I've got to tell you, although I hate to say it, Crystal, with your—er—new—er—friendship with the boss...'

'Don't insult me, Roger, by implying you can't trust me any more.'

'Sorry, Crystal. I didn't mean to cast doubt on your discretion or your principles or whatever, but...' He walked back to the window and stayed there.

'That's OK, Roger,' Crystal encouraged.

'Well,' a long sigh, 'he tried to *bribe* me, Crystal.' A fraught pause. 'If I delivered up to him, he said, the formula of Peach*fleur*, so that they could use it as the basis of their new product—he said they'd got a name: Velvette, would you believe?——' he made a face over his shoulder '—he—well, Halmanner Beauty Products— would give me a lot of money. He told me how much.' He mentioned an amount, and Crystal gasped. 'It staggered me, too.'

Crystal's heart began to hammer, the apprehension she had felt earlier returning but doubled in size. She hardly dared to ask, 'Did you? Accept, I mean?'

'No.' He let out another sigh, of relief rather than disappointment. Crystal sighed, too, with thankfulness that Roger had had the strength of mind to turn down such an offer.

'Roger, I'm so glad! I don't know what the future holds for us job-wise, but I'm certain that if you'd agreed not only would your future have been ruined, degree or no degree, but I'm sure that Shirley's and mine would have been, too.'

It was the second knock on the door that had her spinning on the spot. 'Shirley?' she asked Roger.

'Nope. I left her fast asleep. Crystal, she and I, we're getting on fine. I like her a lot, and she me. You don't mind, do you?'

The knock came again as Crystal was smiling her approval and happiness at hearing the news.

The man standing outside, arms folded, legs belligerently apart and, all told, heartbreakingly attractive, wore a smile that turned her heart over, but which, as she realised her predicament, went into an uncontrollable spin. What would he make of Roger's presence there? A couple of steps and he was in the room.

'For God's sake, Crystal,' Brent was smiling, reaching out for her, 'why did you——?' His gaze slid past her, his hand dropping to his side.

He nodded at Roger, his face a mask. 'Betts.' He looked from one to the other. 'Let me congratulate you...both on your achievements over the past few months. You've done a good job, all of you.'

The words sounded reasonable enough, delivered as they were by a businessman dressed in a business suit and in a businesslike fashion and whose demeanour, in a few biting seconds, had undergone a change from ardent, demanding lover to searing-eyed enemy.

He spun on his heel and left, swinging round outside in the corridor. 'Now I know,' he rasped, 'why you left in such a hurry and without a word.'

As he swung away, the contempt and fury in his gaze hit Crystal like the lash of a whip. Inside her a scream rose up at the terrible pain he had just inflicted and which, she knew without a shadow of a doubt, would remain with her for the rest of her days.

CHAPTER TWELVE

HOME had seemed a million miles away as Crystal had sat in the rear seat of Roger's new car. Shirley had sat beside him and, to Crystal's relief, they had chatted for most of the way.

'We won't come in, thanks,' Shirley said when Crystal invited them. 'I don't know about you, but I'm flaked out.'

'Me, too,' Roger echoed. 'See you Monday at the office? I suppose it's still OK for us to go there now our job's finished? The professionals take over the Peach*fleur* promotion at this point, don't they? Or so I gathered.'

It hadn't occurred to Crystal until that moment that they might not be expected—nor even welcomed any more—at the office adjoining Brent's residence.

'You may be right, Roger. All we can do, I suppose, is to go there as usual. If we're thrown out at least we'll know where we stand. If you get me,' she added, managing a laugh and answering their cheery wave as they drove away.

With her box held firmly under her arm, Crystal let herself in, watering the roses again and placing them temporarily in the tiny entrance lobby. After the excitement of the past few hours, the house seemed very quiet.

Now that the Peach*fleur* promotion was behind her, she could relax a little and give some thought to her future. But right now all she wanted to do was to lie on the bed upstairs and cry her eyes out.

The bed was soft and comforting, but the tears wouldn't come. Her restless thoughts ranged over the immediate past. She had gone to breakfast with Roger and Shirley. Across the room from where they had sat, Brent had shared his table with Lula Hayle.

During the meal Lula's hand had rested often on Brent's. Surely, Crystal had agonised, if I can see him, if he cared to turn round, he could see me? Not once had he bothered to search the room for her. It had been as if she didn't exist.

Brent and his companion had finished early. As they had left the dining-room Crystal had watched their progress, hoping against hope that Brent might look for her then, but his back had been resolutely turned, his attention all for his ex-lady-friend—now, perhaps, reinstated in his life?—as he had listened with a smile to a comment she had made.

Roger had been so right in his summing up of the situation. Brent *had* been playing with her. Last night he had felt the need of a woman in his bed. She had been eager and, she now felt ashamed to admit, very willing indeed, and he had taken advantage of that eagerness. To him it had simply been a way of satisfying his masculine appetites. She would now be filed away, becoming a mere name on that 'computer print-out' of addresses that Roger had jokingly referred to.

Wandering into the living-room, she paused, listening, stiffening, all her senses alert. There was a strange feel in the air, almost as if the furniture and the pot-plants were telling her that something was wrong. The breeze caught the curtain and the rear fanlight window banged and rattled, loosened from its restraining arm.

She had gone away for the night and forgotten to close it! Worse, it seemed that someone had broken in, apparently entering in the same fashion as Brent had done a few weeks before. Oh, no, she thought, despairing, another robbery! She stuffed her fist into her mouth, fear gripping her body as her hands began to shake, her mouth dry up like a parched lake.

A fearful look around began to reassure her. Nothing had been touched. None of the ornaments was missing, the pictures were straight, the cushions were in place. Had she been imagining it, after all? Wait a minute— she stared at the floor... There were dusty footsteps on the pile of the carpet, and they led to... *the computer*!

Someone *had* broken in. She felt the evil presence as if it were still there, and she began to tremble again.

Brent! His name shrieked in her head and she dived for the telephone, hearing it ring and ring in his—oh no, empty?—house. As she was about to put down the phone a voice at the other end said sharply, 'Akerman here.'

'Brent; oh, Brent,' the tears were threatening now, those tears that earlier just would not come, 'm-my house, it's—it's——'

'Yes?' more sharply still. 'It's what?'

'Brent,' a whisper now, 'someone's broken in. While— while I was away for the night.'

'It's been ransacked?' There was no sympathy in his voice.

'No.'

'Things have been stolen? Broken, smashed up, like the shop?'

'No. No,' raising her voice a little, 'I don't think anything's missing. It's just——'

'A feeling you've got?' Now his tone was long-suffering.

'Yes.' She sensed she was losing him, his interest was waning. He didn't care about her any more, so why had she called him in the first place? 'No, not just a feeling. There are footmarks, dirty ones. Not mine—too big anyway.'

'Betts?' with cynicism.

'No!' she shrieked. 'An intruder. I *know* it was. They—they lead to the——' it sounded so silly, so stupid, '—the computer.'

The silence was so long that she thought he had gone. Then there was an exclamation and the phone crashed down, leaving her staring at it. Brent, in whose arms she had lain last night and who had made such intimate, such precious, such magnificent love to her had declined to come when she needed him so, had cast her out of his life so ruthlessly that he had refused to come at her call?

Hand to her head, she wondered what to do. Call the police? They would laugh, wouldn't they? Nothing stolen, as far as she could see, nothing disturbed, not even any concrete evidence to present them with, except those dusty footsteps, which any one of her visitors could have left behind.

She glanced abstractedly at Roger's notes, which she had left in an untidy pile after printing them out, intending to bring some order to them on her return. *They had been tidied for her.* But no one, not even the police, would take the statement seriously.

The rap on the door, the imperious ring at the bell had her racing to open it. For a mere second her eyes met Brent's, then he motioned abruptly that he would like to enter.

'Sorry,' she mumbled, standing back as he strode into the room.

'Have you touched anything?'

'Nothing, Brent.'

He looked around. 'How was an entry achieved?' The rattle of the window answered him. 'Crazy of me to have asked.' He half turned, no friendliness, let alone compassion, in his eyes. 'You left it open again?'

Dumbly, she nodded.

'You're certain there's nothing missing? Kitchen? No? Upstairs?'

Crystal shook her head. 'Everything's OK. I would have noticed at once. I—I went up there when I came home to have a—a rest.' I even tried to cry...over you...but no tears came. 'I didn't come in here until just before I phoned you.'

He stared at the footmarks. He seemed to conclude, as she had done, that they led to the computer. His whole manner underwent a change. Suspicion was uppermost in the glance he speared at her.

'For heaven's s-sake, Brent,' she stammered, 'I didn't arrange this. I *discovered* it when I got home.' She backed away. 'Why are you looking at me like that?'

'You and Betts between you—you engineered this.'

White-faced, Crystal stared at him. 'What are you talking about?'

'To cover your tracks. Do you think I don't know what's been going on?'

Bewildered, she shook her head. 'Please tell me what you're getting at.'

'Getting at? I've had my suspicions for weeks. Ever since Betts went to Ornamental Cosmetics' lab.'

Crystal drew a deep, unbelieving breath. So that was it!

'The chemists there,' Brent was saying, 'had their grave doubts about the reason he gave for permission to visit the lab. So he was watched. Every movement he made was picked up on the security video. That shocks you? You were aware from the start, as he was, that the formula of the skin cream——'

'Skin cream formula?' she echoed, aghast. 'But——'

'—the one,' he continued relentlessly, 'you chose to call Peach*fleur*, was a strict secret, and was destined to remain so.'

'I knew that,' she whispered, 'we all did.'

'Thank God it still is. Yet Betts thought he could get away with searching for it with no questions asked?'

'You're so wrong,' Crystal burst out. 'The reason he gave for wanting to see the lab was true.'

'To help him with his studies.' Brent's tone was crushingly cynical.

She nodded vigorously. 'To enable him to absorb the atmosphere of a truly working laboratory, and a commercially based one at that.'

'So you admit you knew about the lab visit.'

'Of course. He told me about it and the reason why. Probably because I was helping him with his notes and he thought I'd be interested.'

The sideways glance he gave her told her that he remained totally unconvinced.

Crystal paled. He didn't really think, did he, that she was in league with Roger in what he, and plainly others, believed was some kind of industrial espionage on Roger's part?

Brent returned to the pile of notes, flicking through them, then turning back to her. 'Do you really want me to spell out why this break-in occurred?'

'Yes, please,' she whispered, wide-eyed with weariness, of spirit more than body, feeling her limbs relaxing just a little, since it had not been a real robbery after all.

His eyes narrowed. 'I'd have more respect for you if you'd stop pretending you're innocent of any intrigue.'

'But I am!' she cried, knowing now that he really did suspect her. Then she paused, horrified, hearing his words played over. 'Intrigue? What intrigue?' She shook her head wildly. 'But there was no intrigue! Roger's honest, Brent, completely above board.' His eyes hardened at her outspoken defence of the man he was convinced she loved.

'Don't give me that!' The words sliced into her. 'You know as well as I do that it was an employee of Halmanner Beauty Products—although you pretended a week ago that you hadn't heard of them—who was

instructed to break in here, knowing you were at th
promotional party, in an attempt to find that formula

The possibility shook Crystal to her core. 'You mean
they thought, hearing from Roger about his degre
studies, that he might have been allowed in on the secre
and that the formula might be hidden away in his notes?

'Still determined to play the innocent, I see,' he brok
in with biting sarcasm. 'And to protect Betts's character

The venom in his tone made her sway. Did he distrus
her, hate her that much?

'It was only yesterday evening,' she declared in
whisper, 'that Roger told that man——'

'Hal Mannering?'

'You know?'

'Oh, yes, I know him, unprincipled opportunist tha
he is.'

'Well, Roger apparently told him—he seemed to b
the kind of man you could confide in——'

'A clever pose on his part.'

Crystal nodded. How could she disagree, havin
spoken to the man herself? 'As I said, Roger told hir
that his girlfriend—one of his woman colleagues,' sh
amended quickly, noting the forbidding line of Brent
lips, 'typed his notes for him. He even gave the man on
business cards.'

He nodded briefly. 'Hence the break-in. You'll mal
a detective yet,' he rasped.

Where was the man she loved so much, who had hel
her so passionately in the night, made love to her s
wonderfully that even now, with this terrible quarr
tearing them apart, the thought of his naked body again
hers made her flesh tingle and burn?

Who could she turn to for help? If she called Roge
asking his permission . . .

'Since between us we seem to have solved the ridd
of this break-in,' Brent said from the door—he w
going, leaving, just like that, as if she were a mere er

ployee?—'it's up to you,' he was saying, 'whether or not you call in the police.'

A faint ringing sound came from somewhere. Puzzled, Crystal listened intently. She never heard her neighbours' telephones. The stone walls dividing them from each other were too thick for such sounds to penetrate.

'Excuse me.' Brent's eyes were on the opened windows of his car. He made for it and, reaching it, his hand shot out to silence the car phone. Crystal followed slowly, watching him as he talked, then quietly, sadly, returned to her house and closed the front door. A few minutes later his car was gone.

The silence he left behind filled her head with the sound of shuddering sobs. They were, it took her moments to realise, coming from her own throat, her own shaking body.

Waking unrefreshed from hours of turning and twisting, Crystal studied her face in the mirror. She saw the ravages left by the misery of the day before, the paleness of her skin that not even a massage with Peach*fleur* had been able to brighten.

There had to be some way, she thought, of getting through to the man. Or had he finally and irrevocably closed his ears and his mind to any explanation she might advance in an effort to clear her name?

She glanced outside, and her heartbeats responded to the fresh hope that was returning like a flowing tide. The telephone—it had taken Brent away from her. Would it now bring him back?

Lifting the phone, she dialled Roger's number, crossing her fingers that he was there. A female voice answered and her heart began to sink, but then she recognised it as belonging to Shirley.

'Hi,' said Shirley, 'how's things?'

'Not——' Crystal's voice caught in her throat. 'I—is Roger there, please?'

'What's wrong, Crystal?' Shirley asked. 'I'm certa
there's something. Here's Roger.'

'Hi, Crystal. What can I do for you? *Is* there son
thing wrong?'

'Y-yes.' She heard his quick breath, almost felt l
concern. 'R-Roger, there was a break-in—here, at r
place. While I was at the Peach*fleur* launch.'

'Crystal, for heaven's sake! Are you on your own'

'This morning I am. As soon as I discovered it y
terday, I rang Brent and he came.'

'That's all right, then.'

'No, it isn't. Roger, Brent's convinced that we, y
and I, are mixed up in an intrigue—the word is his
with Halmanner Beauty Products and *their* new sk
cream.'

'But of course we aren't, Crystal. Haven't you t
him?'

'He won't believe me. Can I—would you mind ve
much if I told him what you told me in my room at t
hotel?'

'About the offer of a bribe? If it's any use to you,
ahead.' He cut into her thanks. 'Was anything taken

'Not a thing. The only clue was a set of dusty sh
prints, making a beeline for—would you believe?—t
computer. And they had a very good look at your note

'My notes? But why?' A pause, then, 'Wait a minu
I'll take a guess. They thought that, because of the degr
course I'm taking, Ornamental had let me in on t
Peach*fleur* formula, and they were so keen to get it th
they even stooped to a spot of burglary. They knew whe
to come, didn't they? I fell right into their trap, did
I, by telling Hal Mannering that you were helping m
et cetera, and even giving him your card?'

'That's what Brent said, Roger.'

'Look, if you're crying…' He gave a small laugh. 'I'
too far away to offer my shoulder, pal, but—kn
something? There's a much better, much tough

shoulder almost on your doorstep. Take my advice, go find it and *use it*.'

'It wouldn't do any good, Roger. He mistrusts me so much now that I don't think he ever wants to set eyes on me again.'

'Want to bet? I saw the way he looked at you yesterday morning when I was in your room at the hotel.'

'That was yesterday, Roger. He hates me now.'

'Yeah? Look, Crystal, if you want me, you know where to find me. PS,' Crystal smiled through her tears, 'if it's any help, you can even tell him about Shirley and me. Now, is that a big concession? Because we've told no one but you so far.'

Slowly, shakily, Crystal replaced the receiver. Should she seek Brent out? She knew the answer, of course— that she would never forgive herself in the years to come if she didn't make one more effort to tell Brent Akerman the truth.

The bicycle ride to his house had never seemed so long, the road so uphill, the wind in her face so breath-robbing. Wheeling the bike into the front garden, she propped it against the wall of the house.

Turning, she saw him, dressed for work but without his jacket, framed by the opened entrance door, staring at her.

'I had to come,' she said.

'Did you?' His tone gave her no encouragement. 'On Betts's behalf, no doubt.'

'Partly. Partly my own.'

'Well?' came curtly from him.

'Would—would you believe me if I could prove to you that Roger, Shirley and I are incorruptible?'

His mouth twisted cynically. 'Won't you come in?'

Politely, coldly, he backed up the invitation with a sweep of his hand, as if she were a salesperson attempting to sell him something he didn't need—worse, didn't want.

In the living-room, she lifted heavy eyes to his, touching her lip to stop it trembling.

'Have you been crying?' he demanded.

Endlessly since you left me yesterday, she thought. 'What if I have?'

'Please sit down.' She chose an armchair and he walked away, then returned. 'Would you tell me why?' As if he were a psychiatrist, trying to draw a patient out!

'Yes, I will,' burst from her. 'It's you—you're the cause! Your whole attitude...'

Brent stiffened. 'What attitude?'

'The way you won't believe me when I tell you the truth.' Her head snapped up. 'The terrible things you've been implying, about my integrity, my character. Even after...' She checked herself. He might not want to be reminded. It had meant nothing to him.

'After?' his tone softer now.

'After the other night,' she whispered.

He stood in front of her, head back, eyes slanted down. 'The other night?'

Oh, God, she thought, surely he hadn't forgotten?

'You—you and I. Or,' her voice rose, 'was it lust on your part? Or course it was! How ingenuous of me to think it could be anything else.'

'Making love to a woman,' he countered, 'doesn't prove to me, or to any man, that that woman is blameless and honest and innocent of collusion.'

His words were true, even if in her case they were totally wrong. But they served to tell her that she was wasting her time, that his mind was closed on the subject. Nevertheless, she would give him her message, then go.

'So you wouldn't believe me, would you,' she challenged, 'if I told you that at the Peach*fleur* launch Roger was offered a bribe by that man Jimmy Miston, on condition that he revealed to Halmanner Beauty Products the formula of Peach*fleur*? And *this* shows how much they wanted it.' She named a sum that made Brent's eyes widen. 'Nor would you believe me if I told you he turned the offer down flat.'

Brent's face remained impassive.

'You wouldn't believe me, either, if I t-told you that, unlike your lady-friend, Lula, I haven't been indulging in a parallel affair with Roger while—while being so, for want of a better word,' with an unaccustomed touch of cynicism, '*friendly* with you.'

He stared at her steadily.

'Nor,' she persisted flatly, 'would you believe me if I told you,' her voice dropped to a whisper again, 'that, whatever Roger might have felt for me, I've never felt anything but friendship for him.'

'No? You told my sister that you had "someone else, a colleague", who I naturally assumed was Betts.'

'So you did overhear us talking on the day of the picnic!'

'Not intentionally. I was walking towards the kitchen and happened to hear what you said.'

'I only told Mina that to put her off the scent just after she'd told me about what happened between you and Lula.'

He made no comment. When *would* he start to unbend, to give even the faintest sign that he was beginning to change his mind about her, about the whole sorry situation?

'Also,' she made a final effort to prove her own innocence, 'you may or may not believe me, but you've only got to ask them to verify it, and that is that Shirley likes Roger, and Roger likes her a lot, and they've got together. Which for them,' she could not eradicate the bitterness, 'constitutes a h-happy ending.'

Her own words told her how unhappy was her own 'ending' where this man was concerned, which, despite all her efforts to remain composed, set off the tears again.

'Crystal.' She would not look at him, searching instead for a handkerchief. '*Crystal*!' It was an order, from the man who was her boss. 'Wouldn't I? Wouldn't I believe you?'

There was a note in his voice that had her head lifting, her eyes seeking his, being dazzled by the light they held.

'Crystal.' A whisper, then two arms opened wide. Their invitation could not be mistaken. She recalled Roger's advice, to use the shoulder that was there, practically on her doorstep. Those uplifted arms were so familiar, the action so sweet—and so longed for that, in spite of herself, she ran into them...and sobbed her heart out.

Brent held her for a long time, his embrace a comfort, a balm—but, since he was the cause of her distress through his relentless condemnation of her, his accusations that still rang in her ears, it brought her no comfort at all.

He and Lula had got together again—they must have. Hadn't he joined her for breakfast? Hadn't her behaviour towards him been familiar, intimate almost, and his to her tolerant and amused?

This comfort he was offering was based on sympathy for her plight, nothing more.

She pulled out of his arms and raked in her pocket for a handkerchief. Her hand was being opened, and a soft cotton square was placed in it. It was an action she had come to know so well. She started to use it, but it was taken from her. Her chin was tipped, but she closed her eyes, refusing to look at the face that only a few minutes earlier had been transformed with a fury so cold that she felt she had never met its owner before.

'Crystal!' There was that tone again, sharp, brooking no refusal. Where was the softness she so loved, the warmth, the compassion? 'Look at me.'

'No,' she answered thickly. 'I don't want to see your terrible anger. Especially as it's quite unjustified. I'm...we're...completely innocent of your accusations.'

Her eyelids fluttered open, but she continued to stare down. Her chin was given a shake and she was forced to look at him. His expression was beyond her powers to interpret.

'Will you,' she asked his tie, 'listen while I tell you the truth about Roger's visit to the lab?'

'I might.' He released her chin, and with deft fingers he removed his tie as if it irritated him beyond words, then a couple of shirt buttons were unfastened. 'Will you look at *me* now?'

Tears shimmered still as she raised her eyes to his.

'Crystal Rose, for God's sake, stop crying!'

That tone, that ravaged look on his face! What did they mean? Did they have *any* meaning?

'Why shouldn't I cry?' her fretful voice enquired. 'What does it matter to you that I'm upset? I mean nothing to you,' she needed a breath for the lie, 'nor you to me. Your feelings these days, you told me once, are in cold store, and there, you said, they're going to stay. You also said once——'

'What a fantastic memory you have,' he mocked, 'for the meaningless remark.'

'You *meant* every word,' she declared, eyes flashing, 'I'm sure of that.'

'So what did I say?' With a long-suffering sigh he folded his arms and leant against the sofa.

'That where the act of love was concerned these days you simply followed your masculine instincts. Which means that... that the *lovemaking*, except that I'm sure you'd have a much more clinical description for it——'

'How cynical she's getting!' he commented drily.

'—between us was nothing more on your part than a male reflex to—to female sexual attributes.'

Head back, Brent laughed sardonically.

'In any case,' Crystal persisted, 'you've got Lula Hayle, and——'

'Will you tell me whatever it was you were going to tell me?' The anger was back, but instead of upsetting her this time it acted as a challenge.

It came pouring out—how Roger had indeed gone to the laboratory, but for the purely innocent reason that she went on to explain.

'It had nothing whatever to do with finding the formula. If it had he'd have asked outright to see it, wouldn't he, and would have expected a refusal?' He had known all along, she told him, as they all had, that the formula was a secret.

All through the explanation Brent had stared out at the busy street, his ramrod-straight back giving her no clue to his reaction, nor even as to whether he believed her.

'Thank you for listening to me.' Crystal stood up. 'Now you can go back to your precious lady-friend.'

He turned slowly, leaning back against the sill. 'Is that what you want me to do?'

No, a voice inside her shrieked. 'You and she,' she managed with a false calm, 'you've made up your quarrel, haven't you? I could see that over breakfast this morning.'

'You could? Then you must have X-ray eyes. You could see through my back to my thoughts? Through my ribs to my...heart?'

'Your—your heart?' Why was he staring at her like that? 'Your *heart*? What use is that to any woman? It's made of ice.'

He moved quickly, coming round the sofa and seizing her hand, putting it through the opening of his shirt.

'Feel it,' he commanded. 'Is it cold?'

'No.' Summoning her strength, she succeeded in re moving her hand. 'But it isn't warm for *me*.' Head back she threw at him, 'Why don't you admit that it burn for Lula Hayle? She's here somewhere, I'm certain sh is. In your bedroom, probably, dressing for the day, in tending to follow you to your work.' Oh, heavens, she thought, have I gone too far?

Head threateningly low, he approached. 'Nice try, Miss Rose, to cast me in the role of licentious, amoral playboy, but it's a non-starter. I could——' His fingers curled as they moved towards her throat.

'Well,' defensively now, '*you* as good as accused me of duplicity where *my* morals were concerned, implying that I was having an intimate relationship with Roger at the same time as making love with you.'

'*Touché*. OK,' he walked away, came back, 'so past experience embittered me where women were concerned. Lula Hayle let me down so badly that it's taken me years to change my view of her sex.'

'Your sister told me,' she offered quietly.

He seemed drawn to the window, staring at the flowers. 'Why did you shut the door on me last night?'

She was genuinely puzzled. 'What do you mean?'

'You followed me out to the car. I finished the phone call, but you had gone.'

'I——' Should she risk it? Shouldn't she, she asked herself, let sleeping anger lie? 'I didn't think you'd want someone you mistrusted so much to overhear your call.'

Brent drew in a hissing breath and looked sharply over his shoulder. 'Gentle and tender on the surface you may be, but you know how to draw blood.'

'I'm sorry,' she whispered, and she was. She should never have tried to hurt him, because in doing so she had hurt herself too. 'Would you have come back?'

'I'd have come back.'

How she wished he had!

'I gave you red roses with that crystal bowl,' he reminded her. 'What message are they supposed to convey?'

It took her a full ten seconds to recover her breath sufficiently to answer, 'A message . . . of love?'

'Exactly. A message of love.'

'Oh, Brent, I——' He hadn't turned, yet she longed to run into his arms. Was there something she could say to reinstate his belief in womankind...most of all, *in her*?

It was a precious secret, but if she didn't tell him now, even though his back was so daunting that she wanted to pound it with her fists, the chance would be lost forever.

'Brent, I could never have loved Roger.' Her voice rose a little. She was beginning to despair that she would ever get through to him. 'You see, I'd fallen in love with...with someone else.'

There was a sharp movement from the man at the window. 'Name him,' he said, his tone raw.

She had paused too long, it seemed, since he swung round, with three strides confronting her, seizing her elbows and jerking her against him.

Her head went back, the better to look at him, her auburn hair hanging down, picking up the lights from the afternoon sun.

'A—a man called Brent Akerman,' she whispered then hid her face against him. He didn't stir, and for a terrible moment she thought she had embarrassed him so much that he would turn and leave.

Then, with a convulsive movement, his arms wrapped around her. 'Thank God I've got it out of you,' he breathed into her hair.

'Brent,' unbelievingly, 'is it the same with you?'

'The very same,' with a catch in his voice.

'Since when?' she whispered.

'Since when do you think? The first time I set eyes on you, when I was jet lagged and tired to my bones.' He held her away, the better to look at her too. 'Believe me, seeing you appear on my particular scene that evening was like a vision materialising, a piece of a dream taking on a beautiful, unbelievable substance.'

'And I—I expect you'll laugh, but... I was convinced I'd seen *you* somewhere before. I had—in *my* dreams. So you see, I know it sounds impossible, but I loved you even before I met you.'

'Snap, Miss Rose.' He drew her down on to the sofa. 'When I woke up that night after we'd met again at that meeting, and found myself in your house, with you looking at me in that special way you have—I thought my birthday had come early. You, my own, with your fiery rebellion alternating with delicious submission— the kind a man loves in a woman—in the right place and at the right time; your fire and your calming powers, two people in one. When we marry——'

'Marry?'

'That's what I said. Marry,' he stated firmly. 'Say yes, or I'll——'

'Oh, yes, Brent, yes! But——' he growled at her prevarication '—please tell me if you really mean what you're saying. You see, your sister Mina——' he groaned now, burying his face in her neck '—told me you once said that after Lula you'd never propose marriage to any woman again.'

'That, my little peachflower,' he lifted his head, eyes blazing with impatience mixed potently with desire, 'was before I met you. One glance was enough to undo my bad—I won't say good—resolution.' He held her eyes. 'Listen carefully, Crystal Rose. I'm tying you to me, by ceremony and contract, so tightly that you'll never be able to escape. Any objections? Because if so, speak now or, as they say, forever hold your peace.'

'None at all, but even if I was to object,' Crystal smiled, head on one side, 'I'm sure you'd overrule it.'

'Dead right. What I feel for you, Crystal, I've never felt before for any woman.'

'Not even Lula?'

'Not Lula. It would have been the biggest mistake of my life. Whatever you might think, my love, she doesn't

figure in it now, nor has she for years. Why do you think
I took *you* to look at Wayland Cottage?'

'Because one day you knew—hoped——?'

'Knew,' he interposed. 'No question about it.'

'And all the time I thought it was Lula you intended
to install there.'

He shook his head firmly. 'Oh, no. Never!'

'Will you tell me something, Brent?' His raised brows
invited her to continue. 'How long was I under
suspicion?'

'Of being in collusion with Betts?' His expression
underwent a subtle change. It was Brent Akerman, the
businessman, talking, and Crystal found she didn't like
that at all. He shrugged. 'He should have told them outright that there was no question of his being after the
formula.'

'He honestly had no evil intentions in going to the lab.
Which means that there wasn't anything for me to be in
league with him about. Do you believe me now?'

He looked at her, and she saw with a giant leap of
her heart that the Brent she loved so much was back.
And that he did believe her, after all.

'I fell for you, Crystal Rose, body and soul.'

'Even though for a long time you didn't entirely trust
me?'

'My heart trusted you.'

'But it had turned to ice.'

'You melted it.' He kissed the tip of her nose. 'Did I
forget to tell you? But my reason told my emotions to
proceed with caution.' With a smile he added, 'Needless
to say, for once I disregarded its warning.'

'If I'd been guilty, that would you have done?' Was
she delving too far into his private feelings? He'd warned
her once never to let him down.

He growled against her ear, 'What would I have done?
Throttled you, I expect. Then made merciless love to
you—like this.'

He lifted her to lie full-length on the sofa, and piece by piece he disposed of her coverings. Then, tearing off his shirt, he placed himself beside her, his mouth making speech virtually impossible. All the same, there was something she had to say to him before she lost herself in him.

'Brent?'

'For heaven's sake, woman,' with an indignant impatience, 'can't it wait?'

'It's very important. To me, anyway.'

'OK.' He sighed against her cleft, his lips and his tongue bringing little gasps to her throat.

'Once, Brent, when you were at my house, you whistled that song—it's a poem really.

'There is a lady...'

He took her up.

'...sweet and kind,
Was never face,'

he kissed her eyes, her forehead, her mouth;

'so pleased my mind...'

'You never finished it, and I so wanted you to that day. Will you finish it now?'

'Oh, yes, I'll finish it...

'But change the earth or change the sky, yet will I love her till I die.'

She sighed. 'Thank you, Brent. I've waited a long time for those last few words.'

He laughed, his hand trailing over the skin of her stomach and creeping down and down, creating havoc with her very feminine reflexes. 'And I've waited a long time for this, Crystal Rose. Ever since yesterday morning when I reached out to take you in my arms and make love to you all over again, and found you'd gone. Now will you let me——?'

'Brent?'

'No more interruptions.'

But she persisted with a provocative smile, 'Are you jet lagged?'

It was a joke, a secret they shared. Recognising it, he lifted his head again, eyes glinting.

'The only journey I've made these past few hours has been the long, long journey to you. *Jet lagged*?' He pretended to be outraged. 'Are you, by any chance, challenging my erotic staying power?' He looked around. 'Not here. Come up to my bedroom, my love, and you'll discover the answer to that question.'

Gathering up her slender form, he swept her up the stairs, the cool air fanning her skin from head to foot and making her press herself against him for warmth.

Laughter rumbled beneath his ribs and his head came down, capturing her mouth, neither of them releasing it when they reached his room. A few minutes later, responding with wild abandon to the passionate strength of his demands, she found that the answer to her question was a very satisfactory one indeed.

A long while later she stirred in his arms.

'Brent, darling?'

'Yes?' drowsily, his lips on her hair, her throat, her breasts.

'I have to tell you,' she whispered, her body tingling with the delicious resurgence of desire his intimate attentions were arousing within her, 'my emotional bank account—it's in credit at last. In fact, it's full to overflowing.'

'Mine, too,' he growled, his lips growing more demanding.

Crystal moved away a little and held his eyes, smiling impishly into them. 'My account books are all in order. You're welcome to inspect my figures any time.'

'I'm doing that right now,' he remarked with a wicked gleam. 'And it all adds up to everything a man could ever want in the woman he loves. Now,' huskily, but with a patience that was plainly sorely tried, 'will you please stop talking and let me love you all over again?'

He hauled her back into his arms, and this time she had no difficulty at all in complying with his command.

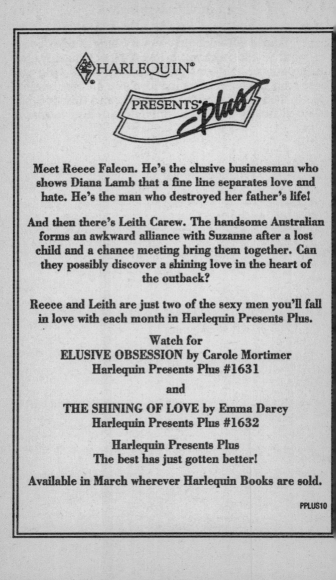

**Fifty red-blooded, white-hot, true-blue hunks
from every State in the Union!**

Look for MEN MADE IN AMERICA! Written by some
of our most poplar authors, these stories feature fifty of
the strongest, sexiest men, each from a different state in
the union!

Two titles available every other month at your favorite
retail outlet.

In March, look for:

TANGLED LIES by Anne Stuart (Hawaii)
ROGUE'S VALLEY by Kathleen Creighton (Idaho)

In May, look for:

LOVE BY PROXY by Diana Palmer (Illinois)
POSSIBLES by Lass Small (Indiana)

You won't be able to resist MEN MADE IN AMERICA!

HARLEQUIN®

Don't miss these Harlequin favorites by some of our most distinguished authors!
And now, you can receive a discount by ordering two or more titles!

HT#25409	THE NIGHT IN SHINING ARMOR by JoAnn Ross	$2.99 ☐
HT#25471	LOVESTORM by JoAnn Ross	$2.99 ☐
HP#11463	THE WEDDING by Emma Darcy	$2.89 ☐
HP#11592	THE LAST GRAND PASSION by Emma Darcy	$2.99 ☐
HR#03188	DOUBLY DELICIOUS by Emma Goldrick	$2.89 ☐
HR#03248	SAFE IN MY HEART by Leigh Michaels	$2.89 ☐
HS#70464	CHILDREN OF THE HEART by Sally Garrett	$3.25 ☐
HS#70524	STRING OF MIRACLES by Sally Garrett	$3.39 ☐
HS#70500	THE SILENCE OF MIDNIGHT by Karen Young	$3.39 ☐
HI#22178	SCHOOL FOR SPIES by Vickie York	$2.79 ☐
HI#22212	DANGEROUS VINTAGE by Laura Pender	$2.89 ☐
HI#22219	TORCH JOB by Patricia Rosemoor	$2.89 ☐
HAR#16459	MACKENZIE'S BABY by Anne McAllister	$3.39 ☐
HAR#16466	A COWBOY FOR CHRISTMAS by Anne McAllister	$3.39 ☐
HAR#16462	THE PIRATE AND HIS LADY by Margaret St. George	$3.39 ☐
HAR#16477	THE LAST REAL MAN by Rebecca Flanders	$3.39 ☐
HH#28704	A CORNER OF HEAVEN by Theresa Michaels	$3.99 ☐
HH#28707	LIGHT ON THE MOUNTAIN by Maura Seger	$3.99 ☐

Harlequin Promotional Titles

#83247	YESTERDAY COMES TOMORROW by Rebecca Flanders	$4.99 ☐
#83257	MY VALENTINE 1993	$4.99 ☐
	(short-story collection featuring Anne Stuart, Judith Arnold, Anne McAllister, Linda Randall Wisdom)	

(limited quantities available on certain titles)

	AMOUNT	$
DEDUCT:	10% DISCOUNT FOR 2+ BOOKS	$
ADD:	POSTAGE & HANDLING	$
	($1.00 for one book, 50¢ for each additional)	
	APPLICABLE TAXES*	$ _____
	TOTAL PAYABLE	$ _____
	(check or money order—please do not send cash)	

To order, complete this form and send it, along with a check or money order for the total above, payable to Harlequin Books, to: **In the U.S.:** 3010 Walden Avenue, P.O. Box 9047, Buffalo, NY 14269-9047; **In Canada:** P.O. Box 613, Fort Erie, Ontario, L2A 5X3.

Name: _____

Address: _____ City: _____

State/Prov.: _____ Zip/Postal Code: _____

*New York residents remit applicable sales taxes.
Canadian residents remit applicable GST and provincial taxes.

HBACK-JM